ghosts in the attic
The Haunted Hearts Series
Book Three

lia lucas

Ghosts in the Attic
The Haunted Hearts Series - Book 3
Copyright © 2024 by Lia Lucas
All rights reserved.

Book Cover and formatting provided by Trisha Fuentes
https://bit.ly/m/trishafuentes

No part of this book may be reproduced in any form or by any electronic or mechanical means, including information storage and retrieval systems, without written permission from the author, except for the use of brief quotations in a book review.

ISBN: 979-8-3305-3208-7 (Paperback)

Published by
Ardent Artist Books
www.ardentartistbooks.com

about ardent artist books

➥ **ABOUT US**

Ardent Artist Books was established in 2008

We publish modern and historical romances once a month!

Get Your FREE List: Published & Upcoming Books
visit our website at:
https://bit.ly/3Wva4o0

➥ **WE HAVE BOOK TRAILERS**

Follow us on YouTube!
https://bit.ly/3W3xn7a

Like, Subscribe & Comment

➥ WE HAVE SERIALIZED FICTION!

Visit our website today to download one of our stories that unfold in bite-sized pieces!

Each installment is just 99¢!

https://bit.ly/3LsDpJL

➥ LET'S CONNECT!

Fuel your love of fiction with exclusive content and captivating insights from Ardent Artist Books. Whether you crave the thrill of modern narratives or the timeless elegance of historical fiction, our newsletter delivers a curated selection straight to your inbox. Plus, as a welcome gift, receive a FREE downloadable eBook:

"The Family Fix"
https://bit.ly/49BR3UB

contents

1. Arrival at the Delgado House — 1
2. Whispers in the Attic — 11
3. Ghostly Discoveries — 21
4. The Story Unfolds — 29
5. Reflection — 39
6. Back to School — 49
7. The Witch's Legacy — 59
8. Nighttime — 67
9. Who Are You? — 75
10. Listen To Me — 83
11. Chaos — 93
12. Love Entwined — 99

Journey to Crystal Lake - Part One — 105
Haunted Hearts — 107
About Lia — 109
Also by Lia — 111

1
arrival at the delgado house

The small town of Willow Creek sparkled in the late afternoon sun, with its quaint streets lined by trees bursting with early autumn colors. Word of the upcoming harvest festival animated the community. People buzzed about, chatting with neighbors and children darting between vendors setting up stalls, ready to sell homemade jams and hand-knit scarves. The air was sweet with the scent of apple cider and caramel corn, making Carson's heart swell with a sense of belonging.

Approaching the Delgado home, she couldn't help but admire its architectural beauty. The Victorian house stood majestically, its striking burgundy and cream façade glowing as the golden light cascaded over it. Ornate gables reached toward the sky, and the wrap-around porch, with its spindled railings, invited questioning fingers to roam the smooth, aged wood. Each step on the creaking floorboards whispered stories of the past, and Carson felt an unexplainable thrill as she entered the world of her best friend.

"Carson!" Milly's voice rang out like a sweet melody, and before Carson could step through the doorway, Milly rushed forward, arms wide in enthusiastic welcome. The two embraced tightly, laughter echoing through the airy foyer as Milly spun Carson playfully.

"Did I miss you, or did you just get taller?" Milly teased, a smirk pulling at the corners of her lips as she pulled back to inspect Carson's face.

"You're just shrinking," Carson shot back, the stickiness of their friendship weaving the words together.

"No way! I'm just focusing on growing the personality!" Milly struck a pose, her long black hair flowing theatrically behind her.

Grinning, Carson stepped into the Delgado home, letting the warmth wash over her. The cozy spaces blended modern and vintage styles, a reflection of Milly's creative family. Soft couches nestled next to rustic coffee tables, while their vibrant artworks adorned the walls, telling stories of the past and hinting at family love.

Carson settled onto the overstuffed couch, sinking into the cushions as Milly flopped beside her, radiating energy. "So, have you been asked to the Winter Formal yet?"

The question caught Carson off guard. Winter Formal? The annual dance felt like light-years away, something she hadn't even thought about. "Nope, not yet." She shrugged, casual, though anxiety prickled at her edges. "What about you?"

Milly's expressive dark brown eyes lit up with mischief. "Oh, you're gonna die when you hear this! Shawn Estevez asked me last night!"

Carson's heart raced. Shawn was popular — the kind of guy who turned heads and had the kind of smile that lit up the whole room. Her excitement bubbled over, and she let out a little squeal, clapping her hands. "No way! That's amazing! You and Shawn? You have to show him your dance moves!"

Milly sunk back into the cushions, a dreamy expression on her face. "Right? I told him I'd have to give him a masterclass in how to properly show off," she giggled.

Carson chuckled, enjoying the moment but a flicker of longing crossed her mind. She didn't want to dwell on it, and pushed the thought aside. It was Milly's time to shine tonight, not hers.

They both leaned back, basking in the vibrant atmosphere that thrummed with youth and dreams. Their laughter bounced off the walls and settled comfortably between the vintage wallpaper and polished wood floors until an unsettling sound broke through their playful banter.

Thud. Thud.

Milly's laughter faded, and she straightened up, her brows furrowing. "What was that?"

Carson's heart raced again, the laughter stuck in her throat. "I... I don't know."

Thud. Thud. Thud. Thud.

There it was again: a distinct thump followed by a series of echoing footsteps. They seemed to be coming from the attic. The two girls looked at each other, uncertain expressions creeping onto their faces.

"Do you think it's..." Milly trailed off, her voice barely above a whisper. A chill danced across Carson's skin as she nodded slowly. The attic had always held its secrets, the kind of mysteries that made Carson's heart beat faster but also sent a shiver skirting down her spine.

"Yeah," Carson replied, biting her lip. The connection she felt to the spirit world lingered close to the surface, especially in the presence of Milly, who was never skeptical but *always* curious. Carson had sensed the weight of longing and pain that existed in the house before. The house had its stories, and though Milly often teased her about her medium abilities, she'd never doubted the strength of Carson's connection.

"What if…" Milly's voice cut through the thick tension, a mix of fear and intrigue brewing in her eyes. "What if the ghost lovers are at it again?"

Carson's breath caught. "You mean, like, trying to finish their story?" A flicker of hope intertwined with tension appeared in her chest.

Milly leaned forward, excitement coursing through her. "It would be like our very own ghost detective story! They could need our help!"

Just then, another loud bang echoed from above, shaking the very foundation of the house. Their playful mood screeched to a halt, stilled by the gripping question of what awaited them up there.

"Maybe it's your brother?" Carson asked, curious.

"He's not home," Milly replied quickly, "Or, maybe he is—I don't know! Do you wanna go check?" Milly asked, her voice low, eyes darting to the attic door, the very spot that often felt alive with history.

"I don't know…" A mix of thrill and dread swirled inside Carson. "What if it's—"

"Just a raccoon?" Milly interjected, her teasing tone attempting to break the seriousness. "Com'on, let's finally do this! The other times you've been here, you always run away—*com'on*; let's be brave!"

The challenge in Milly's voice stirred something deep within Carson. "Okay, but if we go, we have to be quiet. I don't want to scare them—or whatever it is—away," she replied.

A spark of determination ignited in Milly. "Right! Ghost detective mode activated. Let's go!"

The girls rose from the couch, packing away their earlier joy, its remnants now overshadowed by a shared sense of purpose — and just a dash of fear. They tiptoed toward the staircase, each creak of the old wood heightening the tension in the air.

Milly reached for the doorknob to the attic, her hand trembling slightly. "Okay. On three. One… two… three!"

With a deep breath, they flung the door open, revealing the twisting staircase that spiraled up into shadowy uncertainty. Dust motes glittered in the thin slivers of golden light streaming through the worn window at the top.

A hush fell over them as they climbed, each step a mixture of anticipation and dread. The atmosphere shifted, growing heavier as the faint sounds intensified. Their breaths mingled: quick gasps of excitement and anxiety layered together.

"Do you think we should call for them?" Milly whispered, stepping cautiously onto the wooden landing.

Carson's heart pounded in her chest, but she felt drawn to this inexplicable connection. "No," she replied, taking a step forward.

Light flickered before them, casting shadows that danced along the walls. The attic lay before them, a world frozen in time, untouched by modern renovations. Old trunks and forgotten toys waited like relics of sadness and secrecy.

"Does your mom come up here?" Carson asked, running her hand across the 18th-century furniture.

"Heck-no!" Milly whispered. "She's too chicken... That's why all this old furniture is still here."

Then, an overwhelming wave of energy washed over Carson, pulling at her very being. She stopped just inside the entrance, everything else blurring into oblivion as the air thickened around her.

"Carson?" Milly's voice broke through her concentration, returning awareness to the moment. "Are you okay?"

"I... I feel something," Carson admitted, her voice barely above a whisper. "Like... they're close."

"What do you mean? Like *how* close?"

Carson glanced back and met Milly's eyes. The warmth of their friendship wrapped around her like a shield. The connection was undeniable, and so was the thrill of possibility that lay just beyond their grasp.

"The lovers, Milly. I can feel them here."

The two girls jumped when a shadow appeared at the top of the staircase. The soft sound of footsteps echoed from the hallway. Marty appeared (Milly's twin brother), casually leaning against the door frame, the afternoon light casting halos in his tousled hair.

"Hey, what are you two up to?" He smirked, his warm brown eyes glinting mischievously as he took in the scene.

"Just looking at old photos. Care to join?" Carson quipped, suddenly feeling a jolt of warmth rush through her as their eyes locked.

"Nah, I'll spare myself the embarrassment," he countered, crossing his arms, playful confidence radiating from him.

"Coward!" Milly chimed in, shooting a playful glare at her brother.

"Hey! No one wants to relive the moments of selecting the wrong shirt for school picture day," Marty shot back, a grin stretching across his face.

In that lighthearted banter, Carson felt the pull between her and Marty deepen. Her laugh bubbled up despite her heart fluttering, appreciation growing for how effortlessly their trio vibed with each other.

"So... attic?" Milly said, a conspiratorial glint in her eye while leaning closer to Carson. "You know this attic, right? Hate to be the one to point it out, but I think we have some ghostly activity!"

"I got this," Carson bragged, her voice laced with playful confidence as she ambled around the attic, her fingers gliding over the surface of an ornate candlestick. The cool metal felt smooth beneath her touch, and she admired the intricate designs etched into its body, each swirl and curve telling a story of its own.

"Easy, ghost whisperer. I've got your back," Marty said with a grin, shaking his head as though she had it all wrong.

Carson stepped further into the dim confines of the attic, her heart racing. The creaky wooden floorboards beneath her feet hinted at a wealth of years. Dust danced lazily in the sunlight that trickled through the grimy window, illuminating a treasure trove of forgotten relics. Each item seemed steeped in history, whispering secrets of times long past.

The sight astonished her. Dusty oil lamps lined the narrow window sill, their glass globes etched with delicate patterns that glimmered with the day's remaining light. They looked like sentinels guarding the memories of those who had once lit their wicks and filled the room with their soft glow.

Carson's gaze drifted to a set of center tables, each one unique. Some were adorned with intricate carvings — vines curling lovingly across the polished wood surfaces — while others bore the scars of wear, their edges softened by time. She could almost picture them hosting gatherings, laughter ringing out from joy-filled hearts, and quiet conversations cascading into reminiscences.

Nearby, an antique writing desk caught her eye. Its dark cherry finish gleamed under the light, begging to be explored. Carson imagined letters penned there, thoughts flowed out like the blood of its owners. The desk held stories skeletoned under layers of dust, secrets still waiting for someone to uncover.

"Check this out!" Milly's voice called from the doorway, drawing Carson's attention back. But even as she turned to look, something caught at the edge of Carson's senses, a breath of cold air that sent a shiver down her spine.

"Marty? Are you fooling around?" Milly leaned into the room, casually observing the dust motes swirling in the fading light. But Carson remained transfixed, the uncanny sensation wrapping around her like a cold shroud. She couldn't shake off the weight in the air, the sense that they were not fully alone.

"Carson?" Milly's voice grew distant, almost muffled, as Carson willed her feet to move further into the attic. A thick veil of energy pulled her toward the far wall, where long-neglected bookcases stretched like sentinels. The shelves sagged under the weight of forgotten novels and yellowed papers, the bindings cracked from neglect.

Even as the mundane pulled at her thoughts, Carson felt drawn deeper. Her heart quickened as she ran her fingers along the worn spines of the books, each title a fragment of another life, a world where ghosts imagined their love stories again.

"Have you found anything cool?" Milly broke into her thoughts, peering over her shoulder. "Or is it just a bunch of dust bunnies?"

But Carson didn't answer her. The ghostly feeling intensified, swirling around her like leaves caught in a gust of wind. This presence was different — heavier, more profound than anything she ever encountered. She breathed in sharply, and the air turned thick and electric, prickling her skin with the awareness that the lovers they'd heard about were near.

"Carson?" The urgency in Milly's voice snapped at the edges of her concentration.

"I feel... something. Like," Carson hesitated, her voice barely rising above a whisper, "like they're here." She gestured faintly around the attic, feeling the energy unfurling with each step she took. Her eyes locked onto a pair of chairs stretched out across the room. They were mismatched, yet somehow they complemented one another: one ornate and polished, the other plush but frayed, their fabric whispering of countless moments spent in quiet intimacy.

A sudden chill swept through the air, wrapping its fingers around Carson's throat, constricting it slightly. She swallowed hard, then took a slow, deliberate breath. It felt undeniably personal, as though the spirits were craving attention, yearning for someone to listen to their untold story.

2
whispers in the attic

The Delgado home buzzed with the chaotic sounds of a lively morning: pans clanged against ceramic plates, laughter danced through the air, and the warm aroma of sizzling bacon wrapped around the cozy spaces. Morning sunlight filtered through the large windows, spilling golden light across the kitchen. Dust motes floated lazily, shimmering like tiny fairies caught in a moment of magic.

After spending the night, Carson sat at the spacious wooden table, her gaze flickering from the cheerful chaos to the bright patterns of sunlight reflecting off the glass. She leaned back in her chair, a faint smile playing on her lips as the familiar rhythm of Milly and Marty unfolded around her.

Milly leaned forward, energetic and spirited, her long, dark hair swinging as she animatedly recounted how she'd misplaced her favorite pair of sneakers. "I swear, they have legs of their own! They probably escaped out the backdoor to avoid another one of my fashion critiques!"

Marty rolled his eyes, his relaxed charm on full display, as he flipped a pancake onto his plate. "Dude, maybe they just realized they didn't want to be seen in public with you," he teased, making both girls burst into laughter.

Carson felt the warmth of their companionship envelop her, a blanket woven from years of friendship. She leaned against the table, enjoying their playful banter but also absorbing the easy camaraderie that defined Milly and Marty's sibling dynamic.

Despite the lighthearted exchanges, Carson's mind swirled with curiosity. She searched for a moment to dip into the lingering mystery that danced at the edges of her thoughts. Just as Milly leaned back with a triumphant grin over her pancake conquest, their mother, Shannon, walked into the kitchen, her presence radiating a nurturing warmth.

"Mornin', team! What's the verdict on pancakes? Would you call them, perhaps, a culinary masterpiece?" Shannon set a large plate of fluffy pancakes on the table, her voice cheerful and inviting.

"Oh, they're definitely a masterpiece! A work of art!" Milly nodded vigorously, reaching for another pancake before Carson could even respond.

"Totally Michelin star-worthy," Marty chimed in, snickering at Milly's enthusiastic dive into breakfast.

With the atmosphere relaxed and cheerful, Carson took a deep breath. "Hey, Shannon," she started, tucking a stray lock of hair behind her ear. "Can I ask you something about the house?"

Shannon glanced over, her brow slightly raised, intrigued. "Of course, sweetie. What do you want to know?"

"Who used to live here? Like, the original owners? And what about the stories? Milly mentioned some odd noises—like whispers and creaks—since moving in here."

Milly straightened, excitement dancing in her eyes. "Yeah, tell us, Mom! This house has secrets, for sure!"

Shannon chuckled softly, using her spatula to flip a pancake before addressing Carson's question. "This house has quite a history, actually. It was built in the 1700's, I believe. It has been remodeled quite a few times, and we bought it a few years ago. I think the original owners were a family named, 'Crowley'."

Carson's heart raced. "I want to check out the attic later. Alone."

Marty's brows furrowed. "Alone? At that creepy hour? There are ghosts talking up there. I don't want you to get scared and jump out of the attack."

Milly shrugged. "Yeah! I was kind of hoping we could all explore together. You know, like a ghost-hunting squad?"

Carson bit her lip, glancing toward the narrow staircase that led to the attic. "I think I want to go first. By myself," she murmured, feeling a pull inside her chest.

Marty exchanged worried glances with Milly, hesitation lacing his expression.

"Just be careful, alright?" he relented, half-raising a fork of pancake.

As the siblings returned to their playful conversation, Carson felt a wave of determination crash over her. She finished her breakfast, but her mind lingered on the attic.

Carson swirled the last bites of her pancake around her plate, her mind already drifting from the syrupy sweetness to the mysteries that awaited her upstairs. She glanced at Shannon, her curiosity building. There was clearly more to this old house than met the eye.

"Hey, Shannon," Carson began, her voice carrying a hint of hesitation as she chose her words carefully. "How come you've never mentioned anything about the house being...haunted before?" She paused, taking in the slightly surprised expressions from Milly and Marty. "I mean, I've been coming over for a couple of years now, and Milly never said anything about strange noises or whispers."

Shannon set her spatula down, a wistful smile playing across her features. "Well, sweetie, I suppose we didn't want to scare you off!" She chuckled softly. "But in all honesty, I wasn't entirely sure what to make of those stories myself at first."

Milly leaned forward, her dark eyes sparkling with excitement. "Yeah, we didn't want to freak you out until we knew for sure! But now that you've brought it up, you have to tell her about the Crowleys, Mom!"

Shannon nodded, wiping her hands on a dish towel as she settled into the chair next to Carson. "You're right, it's time you heard the whole story." She took a deep breath, her gaze becoming distant as she delved into the history that lingered within these walls.

"The original owners of this house were a young couple named Sebastian and Celina Crowley. From what I've been able to piece together, they lived here in the late 1700s. It was a passionate, forbidden love that faced many obstacles." Shannon's voice took on a wistful quality, her words carrying the weight of the centuries-old tale she was about to unfold.

Carson felt a shiver run down her spine, her medium abilities stirring within her, as if sensing the ghostly presence that had haunted these rooms long before any of them had arrived. She leaned forward, captivated by the prospect of unraveling this mysterious love story.

Shannon continued, her expression solemn. "Legend has it that Sebastian was from a wealthy family, while Celina came from more humble beginnings. Despite the societal divides of the time, they fell deeply in love, drawn to each other like moths to a flame."

Marty, who had been uncharacteristically silent, spoke up, his brow furrowed in contemplation. "But if they loved each other, what happened? Why are they still...here?"

A shadow seemed to pass over Shannon's face as she recounted the tragic events. "From what I understand, their love was met with fierce opposition, particularly from Sebastian's family. There were rumors of a forbidden pregnancy, a secret marriage, and a series of misunderstandings that ultimately led to their untimely deaths."

Carson's heart clenched as the pieces began to fall into place. She could almost feel the weight of their heartbreak, their love torn asunder by forces beyond their control. Her fingers instinctively reached for the charm around her neck, a talisman that had once belonged to her grandmother – a reminder of the enduring power of love, even beyond the veil.

"So, you're saying their ghosts are still here?" Milly's voice was hushed, her eyes wide with a mix of intrigue and apprehension. "Like, they're trapped in the attic or something?"

Shannon nodded solemnly. "That's the legend, at least. People have reported hearing whispers, catching glimpses of shadowy figures, and feeling an overwhelming sense of sadness and longing emanating from the attic over the years."

Carson's mind raced with possibilities, her connection to the spiritual realm pulsing with a newfound urgency. She knew, deep within her core, that she had to uncover the truth behind

Sebastian and Celina's story – not just for her own curiosity, but as a medium, it felt like a calling, a chance to provide closure and peace for these restless souls.

Carson's gaze drifted toward the narrow staircase leading up to the attic, her curiosity piqued. "Shannon, if the house has been remodeled so many times over the years, why was the attic left untouched?"

Shannon followed Carson's line of sight, a thoughtful expression etching across her features. "You know, that's an excellent question. The truth is, every time we considered renovating the attic, there was this inexplicable hesitation, a feeling that we shouldn't disturb that space."

Milly nodded, a mixture of understanding and unease flickering in her eyes. "Yeah, it's almost like something – or *someone* – didn't want us messing with the attic."

A strange silence settled over the kitchen, the weight of Shannon's words hanging in the air. Carson could sense the ghosts of Sebastian and Celina, their presence like a whisper brushing against her skin, urging her to unravel the mysteries that lingered within those dusty rafters.

Marty shifted in his seat, his brow furrowed as he processed the implications. "So, you're saying the attic hasn't been touched because of...supernatural reasons?"

Shannon offered a small shrug, her expression open and earnest. "I can't say for certain, but that's the feeling I've gotten. It's as if the attic is a time capsule, preserving the energy and essence of whatever – or whomever – resides there."

Carson's heart raced with a newfound determination. She knew, without a doubt, that the answers she sought lay within those cobwebbed corners, waiting to be uncovered. With a steadying breath, she pushed her chair back and stood, her hazel eyes alight with resolve.

"Then I think it's time someone took a closer look," she declared, her voice carrying a confidence that belied the nervous flutter in her chest.

Milly's eyes widened, and she reached out to grasp Carson's hand, a silent plea for caution. "Are you sure about this, Carson? We don't know what – or who – might be up there."

Carson squeezed her friend's hand reassuringly, offering a warm smile. "I'll be fine, Milly. You know I have a way with…" She trailed off, glancing around the room as if searching for the right words. "…with beings from the other side."

Marty rose from his seat, his expression a mixture of concern and determination. "If you're going up there, I'm coming with you."

Carson opened her mouth to protest, but Marty held up a hand, his eyes locking with hers in a silent challenge. "No arguments, Carson. You're not facing whatever's in that attic alone."

A flicker of warmth bloomed in Carson's chest at Marty's protective gesture, but she knew this was a journey she needed to take alone – at least initially. Offering him a grateful smile, she gently shook her head.

"I appreciate the concern, Marty, but I need to do this on my own first. If there are spirits lingering up there, they might be more receptive to a single medium than a whole group barging in."

Marty's jaw tensed, but he eventually gave a reluctant nod, his shoulders slumping ever so slightly in defeat. "Alright, but if you need me, I'll be right here."

With a deep, steadying breath, Carson turned her gaze back to the attic stairs, the anticipation thrumming through her veins like a heartbeat. She could feel the pull of the spirits, their whispers dancing at the edges of her consciousness, beckoning her to uncover their secrets.

3
ghostly discoveries

Carson stepped into the attic, a hesitant foot sliding over the threshold. Dust motes danced in the dim light filtering through the small, grimy window. The air felt thick, saturated with the weight of history. It seeped into her skin, filling her with an unshakeable sense of awe and trepidation. Each creak of the old floorboards beneath her Converse echoed like whispers of forgotten times, amplifying the eerie ambiance of the secluded space.

The scent of aged wood and mothballs clung to the air, wrapping around her like a lost memory. Carson inhaled deeply, her heart racing in anticipation of what she would discover. The dim light highlighted the countless shadows cast by the antique furniture and trunks, silent witnesses to bygone years. She stepped further in, closing the door behind her, which blocked out the comfortable laughter of Milly and Marty. Alone now, she felt a tingle of electricity—an undeniable pull—drawing her deeper into the room.

Her curiosity got the better of her, and Carson's fingers brushed over the worn wooden surfaces of trunks that dotted the attic floor. She felt compelled to rummage through the disarray, an unexpected excitement bubbling up within her. Old toys lay scattered like forgotten ghosts, remnants of carefree childhoods long past. A doll's porcelain smile had cracked, while a dusty teddy bear seemed to watch her with one button eye that held a story of its own.

In that moment, as she shuffled through the items, she sensed something shift in the air around her. It felt different—as if invisible eyes had turned their gaze upon her. Carson's heart raced, instinctively aware of the spirits that dwelled within the space. The attic was more than just a relic of the past; it was a portal to something infinitely more profound, where love and heartbreak intertwined with her own reality.

She paused, drawn to a large, ornate trunk in the corner. It stood as a testament to time, its exterior adorned with intricate carvings and curling vines. Carson knelt before it and tugged at the latch, dust swirling in the motion. The trunk creaked open, revealing a trove of treasures hidden inside: faded clothing, lace handkerchiefs, and yellowed photographs capturing smiles that seemed to emerge from another era.

As she rummaged further, her fingers grazed a quilt that lay draped carelessly over a nearby stack of boxes. It felt heavier than expected beneath her hands. Lifting it, she discovered something nestled underneath—a beautifully adorned wooden box, its surface smooth and polished. Carson's breath hitched. It radiated an energy she felt resonating with her.

She gently pried the box open, and within sat a collection of love letters, tied together with a faded ribbon. Carson's heart thumped fervently. The weight of the letters seemed to pulse with emotional energy, calling to her like sirens in the night. She carefully unwrapped the ribbon, and the scent of aged paper wafted through the air, stirring a hunger for understanding in her soul.

As she began reading the letters aloud, love and longing poured from the pages—tales of youthful passion and unyielding heartache, penned in elegant cursive. Each letter captured moments shared in secret, the ink speaking of stolen glances and dreams forbidden by societal expectations.

"Sebastian, my heart aches for you,"

she read, her voice trembling with emotion.

"Every day away feels like an eternity, and I long for the moment when our love can finally be free."

Glimmers of candlelight flickered in response, igniting the shadows around her. The air thickened, and Carson felt the breeze caress her, a sensation both chilling and invigorating. It struck her that she was not alone. She could sense the presence of Sebastian and Celina, their spirits yearning to be heard, to have their story unveiled.

Carson's heart raced as she continued to read, her voice resonating through the attic. The couple spoke of dreams shattered by the world beyond their love. The words, heavy yet beautiful, wrapped around Carson's heart like a warm embrace. Yet, beneath their elegance lay fragility—a tale filled with obstacles, misunderstandings, and the undeniable ache of separation.

With each letter, Carson experienced flashes of visions: a lush garden drenched in rain, Celina's laughter intertwining with the sound of raindrops, their fingers brushing beneath the weight of the moonlight. In those moments, the scents filled her senses—fresh blooms, damp earth, and the faintest trace of a floral perfume. They weren't just stories; they were moments frozen in time, each captivating and haunting.

Her internal conflict grew sharper. On one hand, a thrill coursed through her veins at the realization of witnessing their love firsthand, a privilege she never anticipated. Yet the weight of their unresolved emotions weighed heavily on her heart. Carson clenched the letters tighter, tears prickling at the corners of her eyes. *How could she help them find peace when she struggled with her own feelings?*

"Why am I even here?" she questioned softly, glancing around the attic, her pulse quickening at the thought of backing away. *What if she wasn't strong enough to bear the burden they carried? What if these spectral beings took pieces of her soul with them, leaving her empty in the wake of their lost love?*

As she wrestled with the turmoil inside her, the letters continued to whisper their story, revealing the fragility of Sebastian and Celina's bond woven amidst societal pressures. The words were filled with desperate hope—evidence of true love threatened to be extinguished.

"Please, do not forget me"

one passage read. Carson's heart ached as she considered the implications of those words, a reflection of her own insecurities about Marty—about their own unacknowledged connection.

Suddenly, a soft rustle caught her attention, and Carson turned, her pulse pounding in her ears. Sebastian and Celina materialized before her, ethereal and radiant, their expressions carrying lifetimes of yearning. The air vibrated with their presence, her breath hitching as she found herself staring straight into the depths of their eyes.

"Can you help us?" Sebastian's voice was a gentle, haunting whisper, echoing in her mind.

Sebastian stood before Carson, his ghostly visage both striking and melancholic. His wavy chestnut hair tousled over his forehead, giving him an air of carefree elegance that contrasted with the sorrow etched into his features. Deep-set grey eyes held a mix of wisdom and heartache, capturing the essence of a soul who had faced the trials of love and loss. He wore a historical coat and breeches that had faded from their original vibrant hues, now muted by time and marked with the faint imprints of a long-forgotten existence.

An ethereal glow surrounded Sebastian, accentuating the soft lines of his face and casting his form in a gentle radiance that seemed to emanate from within. Despite his spectral nature, there was an undeniable warmth to his presence, as if the embers of his passion still burned brightly, refusing to be extinguished by the cruelties of fate. He exuded a quiet strength, a charisma that both captivated and comforted those in his presence.

As Carson studied him, she could almost envision the man he had been—a soul full of dreams and aspirations, his heart brimming with the fervor of youth and the promise of a love that knew no bounds. Yet, the weight of his sorrow was palpable, a melancholic aura that clung to him like a veil, a constant reminder of the heartbreak he had endured. In his eyes, Carson glimpsed centuries of longing, a desperate yearning to find solace, to untangle the threads of a story that had been left unfinished.

Celina stepped closer, her gaze imploring and filled with a

longing that resonated deeply within Carson's own heart. "We need to leave this place, but we require your aid."

Celina's essence radiated an ethereal beauty that hinted at her tragic past. Long, flowing tresses the hue of moonlight cascaded in soft waves, framing her delicate face with an otherworldly grace. Her pale complexion seemed to glow faintly, as if illuminated by a soft, internal light that gave her an almost translucent quality. Large, expressive eyes the color of the deepest azure pools gazed at Carson with a mournful intensity, their depths holding centuries of sorrow and longing that tugged at Carson's heartstrings.

Celina's appearance was a striking contrast to the dusty disarray of the attic, her spectral form a vision of elegance amidst the forgotten relics. She wore a tattered white dress that draped gracefully around her slender frame, its gossamer fabric swaying gently like mist with each subtle movement she made. The gown's delicate lace and ribbons were faded by time, yet they clung to her form, accentuating the delicate curves of her figure and adding a touch of whimsy to her somber demeanor.

Despite the ethereal beauty that surrounded her, Celina's expression carried a weight of melancholy that betrayed the depth of her suffering. Her brow was ever so slightly furrowed as if she carried the weight of the world upon her shoulders, and her lips were set in a pensive line that hinted at the countless tears she had shed over the course of her existence. Yet, even in her sorrow, there was a spark of warmth and kindness that shone through, a gentle radiance that drew others to her like moths to a flame.

As she gazed upon Carson, Celina's eyes seemed to hold a silent plea, a desperate longing for understanding and resolution that tugged at the young medium's heart. It was as if she could sense the burden of love and loss that Carson herself carried, forging an unspoken connection between them that transcended the boundaries of life and death. At that moment, Carson felt the weight of Celina's story settle upon her shoulders, a responsibility she had never anticipated but one that she knew she could not turn away from.

A chill ran through her, and instinctively, Carson clutched the letters. Overwhelmed by the emotional weight of their plight and her own buried feelings for Marty, she faced the specters, her mind racing. She had found herself entwined in their story, and it was becoming clearer than ever that the past would guide her present.

The air thickened with expectation as Carson's heart raced. The clutter of the attic melted away, and all that remained was the powerful connection binding their fates together. Carson inhaled, determination igniting within her.

"I will help you… I promise," she whispered, feeling the weight of their emotions resonate within her soul as she stared into their longing gazes. Her journey with them had just begun.

4
the story unfolds

As the dust motes swirled in the weak light streaming through the window, the air around Carson shifted palpably, charged with the presence of the specters before her. Sebastian's melancholic grey eyes pierced through the haze, filled with an urgency that anchored her in the moment. His tall, formidable figure cast an ethereal glow, accentuated by the historical coat draping over his frame like a memory too weighted to shake off.

"We need your help." His voice resonated, echoing against the attic's wooden beams. It carried with it the weight of centuries, the depth of long-held dreams shattered by time. "We've been trapped here for centuries, bound by a curse from a witch who couldn't bear our love."

The gravity of his words wrapped around Carson, squeezing her chest. She felt an instinctive pull towards this ghostly couple, the heartbreak etching itself into her own heart. Beyond his call for help laid a tapestry of suffering that resonated with her—a tragic love that refused to fade, hidden beneath layers of regret.

Celina stepped forward, her luminous beauty almost mesmerizing against the dim attic backdrop. Her flowing dress swayed lightly as she moved, and Carson could feel the warmth radiating from her, despite her spectral nature. "Our love was forbidden," Celina murmured, her voice soft, yet filled with a firm determination. "My family did not accept him. To punish us, the witch trapped our souls in this attic."

Carson blinked, momentarily lost in the ethereal glow surrounding Celina. Beneath the tenderness, a fierce resolve lingered. It struck a chord deep within Carson, triggering memories of her own tangled feelings for Marty. The uncertainty, the fear of societal boundaries, the stakes of unseen barriers—they all tangled in her chest, creating a familiar ache.

"We cannot move on," Celina continued, her voice coaxing Carson back to the present, "cannot find peace, until the curse is broken. We believe you possess the power to help us."

Their plaintive request struck Carson harder than any haunting whispers she had ever felt. She thought of her own struggles—her ability to connect with the spirits often left her burdened. This time, it felt different. This wasn't just about her role as a medium; it was something more profound, more essential. It was about love, tied across time, painfully unfinished.

Sebastian stepped closer, a shadow of heartache etched in the lines of his face. "My family's disdain severed our bond in life, and now it keeps us here, in limbo. We long for closure, not just for ourselves, but for our families."

The room felt colder as his words washed over Carson. Pain reflected in their gazes, illuminating the spectral light that surrounded them. For the first time, she realized just how intertwined their stories were with her own—a knot that somehow bound them all. She heard the lull of the letters in her hands, a reminder of the fragility of love's promise.

"I want to help you break this curse," Carson declared, summoning a newfound strength within her. The words burst forth, ignited by the glow of determination swelling inside her. The weight of their turmoil resonated in her bones, driving her resolve deeper. She stepped closer, intent in her purpose.

As she spoke, the atmosphere around them shifted again. The letters, their rustic ribbon untied and whispering secrets, became the portal to their plea. "Our love story is a part of this town's history," Celina added, a hopeful glimmer brightening her ethereal features. "If we can untangle this curse, it will free us—and perhaps, set our families at peace too."

Those words wrapped around Carson like a warm embrace, igniting a spark of empathy. She couldn't ignore the connection that thrummed within her, the intertwining of past experiences with present emotions. Just as they sought closure, Carson found herself wrestling with her own growing feelings for Marty. *Could she face both their stories—their love and her own?*

The specters continued, their voices rising and falling like an aching melody. "The witch's spell cast a shadow over our love," Sebastian explained, his expression taut with anguish. "We must confront the roots of her jealousy, unravel the truths she twisted against us. Only then can we find the fragments of our souls ripped apart."

Tension filled the attic. The chill deepened, and Carson's heart raced as she sensed the urgency looming like a tempest. Every beat echoed the promise of discovery—this was more than just closure for Sebastian and Celina. This was an opportunity to heal, for all of them.

Carson drew in a steadying breath, feeling the tendrils of their sorrow laced with hope. She, a medium amongst spirits, held the capacity to change the course of fate, to bridge the gap between past and present. "Even if it takes uncovering long-buried secrets," she added, her voice firm. "I promise to uncover the truth and help you find your freedom."

As she stepped closer to the ghostly lovers, her resolve hardened, crystallizing in the air.

"I'm ready for this journey," Carson said, the weight of her convictions pulling her forward, tethering her to their plight. "You deserve to be free of the chains binding you in this attic."

Their gaze, so filled with both desperation and a flickering thread of hope, intertwined with hers, weaving a bond that pulsed with a shared purpose. Together, the currents of the past brushed against the present, a tender embrace tinged with possibility.

In that moment, enveloped in the haunting echoes of their intertwined hearts, Carson felt a powerful resolve course through her veins. This wasn't just a battle against a witch's curse; it was a dance with love, loss, and the unyielding strength of the human spirit.

Carson could feel the weight of their stares, the ghostly couple's longing woven into the fabric of her resolve. But with that fading determination came a swift realization—she needed information. *What was the name of the witch?* She understood the burden of the unknown, especially when it entwined with a history that could ripple back to her own roots.

"Sebastian," she asked, her voice steady yet laced with urgency, "what's the name of the witch who cursed you? If we're going to break the curse, I need to know who I'm dealing with."

Sebastian's expression hardened, shadows flickering through their translucent forms. "Her name was Isolde. Isolde Darkmoor," he said, the name spilling like an incantation that hung in the air between them. His gaze shifted, growing distant as if he was summoning memories too painful to bear. "She was once a part of our lives—an unfortunate soul who let jealousy consume her. The Delgado family is . . . *connected* to her."

Carson felt the floor beneath her shift, like a storm brewing in the distance. The history cascading through the air was thick and tangible; the idea that the Delgado family had entangled roots with this dark witch sent a shudder crawling up her spine. She could feel the intertwining of their fates, pulling tighter and tighter.

"Connected?" she echoed, unsure if the thrill running through her was from curiosity or foreboding. "How?"

Sebastian stepped forward as if the question stirred ancient memories that needed to be shared. "Isolde is a distant relative. She was in love with me ... she was driven by a passion that eventually twisted into rage." His tone dipped, anxiety shadowing his features. "When Celina and I's love blossomed, jealousy turned Isolde against us. In her despair, she conjured a curse that sealed our souls. The shame of her actions runs in the Darkmoor blood, and it may not be easy for anyone from that lineage to face this darkness."

The air around Carson thickened. So many questions swirled in her mind—a whirlwind of disbelief mingled with dread. *How could this be? Was it possible that the roots of her own connection to the supernatural were tangled with the dark secrets of a witch? What were the odds?*

"Can you tell me why she cursed you?" Carson leaned in closer, desperation edging her voice. Understanding the origins of the pain was perhaps the only way to carve out a path forward.

Sebastian sighed deeply, his translucent form shimmering with sorrow. "She found out about us. We planned to marry against the wishes of our families. When she confronted me, I rejected her overtures completely. That rejection was the catalyst. She was consumed by a darkness that twisted her spirit. It clouded her judgment, blinding her to love's true power."

As Carson listened intently, she felt Celina move closer, her sorrow mingling with a glimmer of hope. "Isolde cast a spell requiring our continued suffering. To leave this attic, you must dig into the depths of the past. You may need to confront the tragedy of Isolde, and understand her pain, but be careful—her spirit still lingers around these parts."

"That's . . . a lot to unpack," Carson murmured, her heart pounding as she processed the weight of the information. The past and present spiraled around her, and time felt fluid, existing in a realm where love and rage coiled together.

Sebastian's eyes glinted with understanding. "This journey is not just about us. It's about you, Carson. You must find the strength from within to face this. We need you."

Her heart fluttered with the gravity of his words. Carson took a deep breath, glancing down at the faded bundle of letters still clutched in her hands. These artifacts of love echoed with the pain that surrounded her, bittersweet remnants of a time gone by.

"I'll help you," she finally replied, feeling the warmth of a promise forming in the air. Yet her thoughts lingered on the shadowy specter of Isolde. She had to unravel this madness and navigate the interconnected veins binding their souls.

Even as she came to terms with her determination, a sudden gust of wind stirred in the attic, sending chills cascading down her spine. It flickered through the small opening of the window, whisking through the dusty room and whispering danger, warning of troubles ahead.

Sebastian turned sharply, sensing the change in the atmosphere. Carson's heart raced as the temperature plummeted, shadows dancing in the corners like fleeting nightmares. Celina moved closer to Sebastian, the urgency in her gaze painfully clear. "Isolde knows," she whispered, fear creeping into her voice. "If she senses you're digging into her past, she won't stand idly by. She will fight to keep her secrets hidden."

Their warning pulsed through Carson like an electric shock, raising the hairs on her arms. *What would the witch do to protect herself?* This wasn't just a simple battle against a curse; it was a confrontation against a vengeful spirit driven by rage, and the stakes felt unbearably high.

Sebastian's expression grew stern, the glow of his figure intensifying as the wind howled louder. "You need to act fast, Carson. Isolde's presence is growing stronger. We must unlock the truth now before she tries to thwart our efforts."

A wave of anxiety rushed over Carson, but alongside it, clarity began to unfold. The sense of urgency enveloping her ignited the drive within her. She must connect the dots rapidly if they were ever to break free from the curse shadowing them.

She clutched the letters tighter, forming a plan. "Then let's start with the family records. There has to be something in Milly's house, something about Isolde that can help us understand how to confront her."

As Carson turned to leave the attic, the wind whipped colder, laced with sudden menace. The air shifted rapidly, swirling like a cyclone that reverberated with an ominous hum. The shadows flickered again, reaching out like tendrils desperate to pull her back into the grip of the ghostly realm.

And then came a voice—a dark rasp echoing through the attic like a thunderclap.

Leave my past alone...

5
reflection

Carson descended the narrow, creaking staircase, the weight of the attic's secrets pressing heavily on her shoulders. Each step felt like a push against the clammy air, tantalizing with the potential of revelation yet clouded by doubt. She paused at the bottom, feeling the warmth of the Delgado home wrap around her like a comforting blanket. But inside, a tempest churned.

In the living room, Milly, Marty, and their mother, Shannon, settled around the table, laughter spilling out like sunshine. The soft glow from the chandelier illuminated their faces in a way that made the moment almost magical. Carson tried to focus on the familial warmth radiating from the trio, but the ghostly echoes of Isolde and Sebastian lingered in her mind, whispers of love and despair.

Milly caught her eye and raised an eyebrow, an inquisitive smile spreading across her face. "Hey, are you okay? You've been kind of quiet."

"I'm fine. Just—thinking about stuff." Carson's reply felt hurried and hollow, echoing the turmoil inside her. *What would they think if she spoke about the spirits, about the curse that tied their family to Isolde's tragic story?* Loneliness tugged at her, a desire to bridge the growing chasm between her and her best friend.

Marty leaned back in his chair, looking between the two girls. "You know, we could avoid the attic for the rest of the weekend," he teased, a playful smirk dancing on his lips. "Not everything needs to be haunted."

"Thanks for the vote of confidence, Marty," Carson managed a smile, but it fell short, missing the warmth she sought.

What if finding closure for them can help me too? she thought, horror and hope colliding in her chest. The possibility stirred her emotions, pulling her deeper into the ghostly lovers' story, one drip at a time. Isolde's tale was more than just a history lesson—it was a living, breathing consequence of love gone awry, intertwined with Milly's own family legacy. *Would sharing this knowledge draw them apart instead of bringing them together?* She bit her lip, trapped within the confines of her thoughts.

"Yo, earth to Carson! You in there?" Milly waved a hand in front of her, breaking her reverie.

Startled, Carson blinked away the turbulent visions of the attic. "Yeah, sorry. I'm just... really tired." A lie laced with grains of truth.

Milly crossed her arms, her expression shifting from playful to concerned, her gaze slicing through Carson's facade. "Tired? Or something else? You know you can tell me anything."

As Carson's heart raced, she felt the air grow heavy, panic rising like bile in her throat. The truth clamored to escape, but so did the fear of losing the one person who understood her the most.

Carson's mind drifted to the beginnings of her friendship with Milly, as if replaying a cherished memory. They had met in grade school when Carson's family moved to the small town, her mother's ancestral home. A shy, introspective girl struggling to find her place, Carson's world had shifted with Milly's vibrant arrival.

From that first day, Milly's infectious laughter and fearless spirit drew me in like a moth to a flame. She never shied away from my occasional ghostly encounters, instead embracing them with eager curiosity. While others teased or avoided me, Milly became my steadfast ally, a confidante who understood the complexities of my abilities without judgment.

Over the years, their bond had only deepened, a tapestry woven with shared secrets, inside jokes, and a profound understanding that transcended words. Milly's unwavering support had been Carson's lifeline, a tether to normalcy in a world that often viewed her as an outsider.

How could I possibly hurt her by keeping this a secret? Milly is the one person who has always had my back, no matter what. But this—this is different. This is her family's history, their legacy intertwined with a curse that could shatter everything they know.

Carson's heart ached at the thought of causing her best friend pain or fracturing their sacred bond. It wasn't in her nature to intentionally inflict harm, especially on the person who had stood by her through thick and thin. Yet, the weight of Isolde and Sebastian's story pressed upon her, a responsibility she couldn't ignore.

Her gaze flickered to Marty, his casual laughter and easy grin stirring a storm of emotions within her. The depth of her feelings for him had crept up unexpectedly, like a gentle tide slowly eroding the shoreline of her heart.

How am I supposed to navigate these feelings when I'm already drowning in secrets and supernatural complexities? Marty is Milly's twin, her other half—could I risk disrupting that sacred connection for my own desires?

Carson found herself adrift in a sea of conflicting loyalties, torn between her commitments to the ghostly lovers, her friendship with Milly, and the burgeoning emotions she harbored for Marty. Each path held the potential for hurt, for fractured bonds and shattered trust.

As Milly's concerned gaze bore into her, Carson felt the walls closing in, the truth clawing at her chest, desperate for release. But would voicing her discoveries bring them closer or irreparably drive a wedge between them?

I can't lose them, not like this. Milly and Marty are the anchors in my life, the ones who keep me grounded when the supernatural threatens to sweep me away. But how can I protect them from a truth that's already seeping through the cracks?

Her heart raced, each beat a desperate plea for guidance, for a path that wouldn't unravel the cherished bonds she held so dear. As the silence stretched, Carson found herself caught in a maelstrom of her own making, trapped between the ghosts of the past and the living, breathing connections that defined her present.

Carson's mind drifted to the beginnings of her friendship with Milly, as if replaying a cherished memory. They had met in grade school when Carson's family moved to the small town, her mother's ancestral home. A shy, introspective girl struggling to find her place, Carson's world had shifted with Milly's vibrant arrival.

From that first day, Milly's infectious laughter and fearless spirit drew me in like a moth to a flame. She never shied away from my occasional ghostly encounters, instead embracing them with eager curiosity. While others teased or avoided me, Milly became my steadfast ally, a confidante who understood the complexities of my abilities without judgment.

Over the years, their bond had only deepened, a tapestry woven with shared secrets, inside jokes, and a profound understanding that transcended words. Milly's unwavering support had been Carson's lifeline, a tether to normalcy in a world that often viewed her as an outsider.

How could I possibly hurt her by keeping this a secret? Milly is the one person who has always had my back, no matter what. But this—this is different. This is her family's history, their legacy intertwined with a curse that could shatter everything they know.

Carson's heart ached at the thought of causing her best friend pain or fracturing their sacred bond. It wasn't in her nature to intentionally inflict harm, especially on the person who had stood by her through thick and thin. Yet, the weight of Isolde and Sebastian's story pressed upon her, a responsibility she couldn't ignore.

Her gaze flickered to Marty, his casual laughter and easy grin stirring a storm of emotions within her. The depth of her feelings for him had crept up unexpectedly like a gentle tide slowly eroding the shoreline of her heart.

How am I supposed to navigate these feelings when I'm already drowning in secrets and supernatural complexities? Marty is Milly's twin, her other half —could I risk disrupting that sacred connection for my own desires?

Carson found herself adrift in a sea of conflicting loyalties, torn between her commitments to the ghostly lovers, her friendship with Milly, and the burgeoning emotions she harbored for Marty. Each path held the potential for hurt—for fractured bonds and shattered trust.

As Milly's concerned gaze bore into her, Carson felt the walls closing in, the truth clawing at her chest, desperate for release. But would voicing her discoveries bring them closer or irreparably drive a wedge between them?

I can't lose them, not like this. Milly and Marty are the anchors in my life, the ones who keep me grounded when the supernatural threatens to sweep me away. But how can I protect them from a truth that's already seeping through the cracks?

Her heart raced, each beat a desperate plea for guidance, for a path that wouldn't unravel the cherished bonds she held so dear. As the silence stretched, Carson found herself caught in a maelstrom of her own making, trapped between the ghosts of the past and the living, breathing connections that defined her present.

Marty stood and padded to the kitchen, chuckling to himself about something on the television. The temporarily unoccupied space felt charged, seconds stretching into eternity between the two friends.

"Let's talk," Milly pulled Carson aside, her voice low, determined. They moved out of earshot from Marty and Shannon, finding solace in the cozy nook beside the window.

"Carson, I see it on your face," Milly pressed, searching her friend's hazel eyes with unyielding intensity. "What's bothering you? You can't just keep shutting me out."

Carson hesitated, swallowing hard. Tears of frustration nearly escaped her as she fought with herself. The urge to confide battled fiercely against apprehension.

Finally, she blurted, "Fine! You want to know? I—I found some letters in the attic. They belonged to a couple who were, um, in love. But they couldn't be together, and there's a curse. A witch trapped their souls, and—" Carson paused, letting the weight of each word settle in the air around them. "The witch's name is Isolde Darkmoor ... and she's involved with your family, Milly. Isolde—she's cursed and connected to the Delgado lineage. I felt them. They're trapped! And I don't know how to help them!"

Milly's eyes widened, a kaleidoscope of confusion, shock, and sorrow dancing across her features. "What? Celina and Sebastian? But... How does that connect to us? My family hasn't mentioned them."

Carson pressed her lips together, fear gnawing at her. "Maybe it's an old story they don't want to talk about? I haven't figured it all out yet, but I sensed Celina's pain. It mirrors my own... in some way. Love turned into obsession. It's haunting."

The room felt stifling, the weight of Carson's words hanging thick between them.

Milly inhaled sharply, searching Carson's face for clarity, holding her breath as though the act could summon answers. "We have to look into this. You have to show me what you found—I have to tell my—"

A soft creak seeping from the hallway jolted them from their conversation. The sound echoed like a whisper from another time, sending shivers down Carson's spine, the past clawing its way into the present.

"Mom?" Marty called from the other room, but it wasn't his voice that silenced their discussion.

Sebastian emerged, his ethereal figure shimmering just beyond the door, fragile and desperate. He locked eyes with Carson, an intensity radiating from his gaze that pulled her breath away.

"We need your help," he intoned, voice resonating with remnants of lost love.

Milly turned, stunned into silence. Their world twisted frantically as the ghostly plea echoed in her ears.

"What?" Carson gasped, panic sparking in her chest, unsure of how to guide this unexpected encounter. "Did you see him?"

6
back to school

Carson woke up Monday morning with a knot of excitement and anxiety twisting in her stomach. She stared at the ceiling, feeling the weight of the weekend pressing down on her. Today was the day she would see Marty again, and that thought sent shivers through her. He and Milly had always held a special place in her heart, but ever since their revelation in the attic, she felt an electric pull towards him that both thrilled and terrified her.

Her mind drifted back to the haunting story of Sebastian and Celina. The love letters had opened her eyes to how bittersweet romance could be, filled with longing and sacrifice. Their tragic history mirrored her own confusion about Marty and her feelings—he was a bright spot in her otherwise chaotic life, but the ghostly couple's stories loomed, like shadows ready to eclipse her own budding emotions. She thought about how only she had seen Sebastian, while Milly perceived only a whisper that she brushed off as a trick of the TV. It gnawed at her. *If she held this key to understanding the past, how could she keep it from her best friend? How could she navigate her growing attraction to Marty without dragging Milly through shadows?*

Carson pulled herself from bed, readying for school, her heart racing with each step. The day stretched ahead of her, a blend of comfort and turmoil. As she walked through the bustling hallways, echoes of laughter and snippets of conversation washed over her. She noticed a group of jocks nearby, mocking each other over an embarrassing incident from history class, and felt the contrast of their carefree banter against her own heavy thoughts. Her chest tightened.

"Earth to Carson!" Milly's playful voice broke through her reverie as she appeared at her side, grinning wide. "What's got you so deep in thought? Daydreaming again?"

Carson chuckled, but her smile barely masked her swirling emotions. "Something like that," she replied, feeling the weight of the truth lingering just below the surface. They moved through their day together, sharing quick laughs and teasing each other about everything from homework to upcoming tests, but the undercurrent between Carson and Milly about the curse created a tension that made her skin itch.

At lunchtime, they settled at their usual table. The cafeteria was loud, filled with animated chatter and distant laughter echoing around them. Milly picked at her food while exchanging playful banter with Marty, who slid in next to Carson. He ruffled her hair, eliciting an annoyed pout from her that only made him laugh.

"Hey, don't mess up my art project," she mumbled, trying to sound serious but failing as her lips twitched upward.

"Art project? More like a messy catastrophe," Milly chimed in, grinning deviously.

Their sibling dynamic created an easy atmosphere, but it felt like a wall that Carson couldn't break through. She sat between them, sipping her juice and allowing her eyes to drift toward Marty. He caught her gaze suddenly, and a spark ignited in the air—as if the rest of the room faded away. For a moment, all she could hear was the rapid pounding of her heart as they held each other's stares. She sensed the weight of everything unsaid hanging suspended between them.

"Uh, so what's the plan after school?" Marty's voice broke the spell, pulling Carson back to reality.

"Maybe we can go hang out at the arcade?" Milly suggested, a curious glint in her eyes that told Carson she wasn't going to let her deflect any longer. "It'll be fun! We can play air hockey!"

Carson felt a rush of nerves. The love letters still occupied her thoughts. *What if that's what it takes to help Sebastian and Celina find closure?* she thought, balancing on the edge of mixed emotions. They were scattered with whispers of the witch's curse, yet at the forefront of her mind was the undeniable connection forming with Marty.

As the afternoon dragged on, they settled into their seats for a lecture on classic love stories. Carson struggled to pay attention; her heart thudded against her ribcage as the teacher mentioned doomed romances filled with longing. The love letters she found echoed through her mind. She scribbled down her observations, almost as if the act itself would help guide Sebastian and Celina, all while wrestling with the distraction of Marty's presence.

Once the final bell rang, the trio emerged into the cool air together. Milly beamed and nudged Carson lightly. "You're going to tell him, right?"

"What are you talking about?" Carson played dumb but recognized the sinking feeling in her gut.

"About the *Curse of Isolde*," Milly let go in her best creepy baritone voice.

Carson fidgeted with her sleeve, "Milly... it's not that simple."

"Come on! You said he'd understand," Milly pressed, but before Carson could respond, Marty's voice rang out, confidence laced with curiosity.

"What curse?" Marty asked, playfully punching his sister in her arm.

"There's no curse," Carson suddenly blurted out.

"But you said—" Milly cut her off.

"I know what I said—I'll figure it out myself," Carson finalized, walking ahead of the siblings.

Behind Carson, Marty offered, "Well, my grandma used to talk about an old wives tale... She mentioned a relative who dabbled in witchcraft back in the day."

Carson turned around, and exchanged a glance with Milly; eyebrows raised. How had they not heard this before?

"What?" Milly asked, in disbelief.

"I always thought it was just a story," Marty continued, rubbing the back of his neck. "Never actually believed it."

Milly looked at Carson with an encouraging smile. "See? He's already intrigued, Carson."

"Let's just get home first," Carson said, her voice somewhat shaky. She felt the precarious balance of emotions teetering on a tightrope.

"You coming over later? After dinner?" Milly asked, already sure of the answer.

Carson nodded, yes.

AT THE DELGADO HOME, the atmosphere buzzed with anticipation. The familiar, haunting aura encased the old house, thickening in the air. Together, they climbed the narrow staircase leading to the attic, an electric charge enveloping them. Carson noticed erratic shadows dancing at the corners of her vision; the flicker of light bulbs overhead caught her attention, and an unusual shiver traced along her spine.

As they reached the attic door, an ominous gust rushed past them. The door swung shut with a loud bang that echoed in the small space, causing all of them to jump. The unexpected sound brought a surge of adrenaline, forcing them closer together, and Carson felt her heart thrumming louder than before.

"Okay, that was weird," Marty muttered, his brow furrowing as he looked around.

Brushing against Carson, he extended a hand to steady himself. Their fingers brushed for a moment, igniting a spark that sent an electric wave through her. Fear mixed with the undeniable chemistry between them.

A burst of nervous laughter spilled from Milly, breaking the tension. "What's happening?" She tried to play it cool, but her eyes darted between the two of them, clearly reading the dynamics shifting.

"Ghosts, haven't you heard?" Marty joked, but Carson could sense the undercurrent of tension thickening in the air, pulling tighter around them.

As calm returned to the attic, the light flickered again, and the sound of soft whispers filled the space, resonating through the walls. Carson felt a weight pressing down upon her, a sense of urgency that surged through her.

In that moment, she realized that the boundaries between the living and the dead blurred as she felt the ghosts urging her on.

The whispers grew more insistent, their eerie tones sending shivers down Carson's spine. She felt the weight of Isolde's curse hanging heavy in the air, amplifying the supernatural energy that crackled around them.

Suddenly, a shimmering light materialized in the corner, casting strange shadows that danced across the dusty floorboards. Carson's breath caught in her throat as Sebastian's ethereal form took shape before them.

"You brought them," he said, his deep voice reverberating with a haunting resonance that seemed to seep into her very soul.

Carson froze, her eyes fixed on the ghostly figure standing mere feet away. She could sense the centuries of longing and regret that clung to him like a second skin, a palpable aura of melancholy that threatened to overwhelm her.

Beside her, Milly and Marty shifted uncomfortably, their eyes darting from the strange flickering light to Carson's transfixed expression. A crease formed between Milly's brows as she searched the shadows, her gaze filled with a mixture of curiosity and unease.

"Carson, what's going on?" she whispered, her voice trembling ever so slightly.

Before Carson could respond, Marty let out a low whistle, his eyes wide with a peculiar blend of awe and disbelief. "Did you guys see that shadow? Or am I just imagining things?"

Carson's heart raced as she realized the implications of Sebastian's words. Milly and Marty couldn't fully perceive the ghostly figure, their senses limited by the veil separating the living from the dead. It was up to her, with her unique abilities, to bridge that gap and unravel the mysteries that bound Sebastian and Celina to this world.

With a deep breath, Carson focused her energy, willing herself to open her mind and heart to the spirits' plight. She could feel the ghostly lovers' presence surrounding her, their emotions washing over her like waves crashing against the shore.

"You're not imagining things," she finally responded, her voice steadier than she expected. "Sebastian is here, and he needs our help."

Milly's eyes widened, and she instinctively reached for Marty's hand, her fingers intertwining with his as if seeking anchor in the face of the unknown. Marty, ever the protector, squeezed her hand reassuringly, his gaze never leaving Carson's face.

"What does he want from us?" Marty asked, his tone a curious blend of skepticism and genuine interest.

Before Carson could answer, Sebastian's voice echoed through the attic once more. "You must break the curse, or we'll be trapped here forever, doomed to relive our tragic past for all eternity."

A chill ran down Carson's spine as she contemplated the weight of Sebastian's words. Breaking a centuries-old curse would be no easy feat, but she knew in her heart that she had to try. Not just for Sebastian and Celina, but for herself as well – to find the strength to confront her own feelings and forge a path forward, unburdened by the ghosts of the past.

Turning to face her friends, Carson took a deep breath, her eyes shining with determination. "We have to help them," she said firmly, her voice carrying a conviction that belied her inner turmoil.

Milly and Marty exchanged a glance, a silent conversation passing between them that spoke volumes about their unwavering trust and support for Carson. Finally, Milly nodded, a small smile playing at the corners of her lips.

"Okay," she said, her voice filled with the same resolve that burned within Carson's heart. "What do we need to do?"

As the words left her lips, a sudden gust of wind swept through the attic, sending dust and debris swirling around them in a whirlwind of energy. The flickering light intensified, casting eerie shadows that danced across the walls—as if the very spirits themselves were rejoicing at the prospect of their freedom.

But just as quickly as it began, the whirlwind dissipated, leaving a deafening silence in its wake. Carson's heart pounded in her chest as she searched the shadows for any sign of Sebastian or the other ghostly presence that haunted this place.

Suddenly, a faint whisper drifted through the air, its source indiscernible, yet its message as clear as day:

"The witch's legacy... Find the truth within..."

7
the witch's legacy

Carson woke up as morning light crept into her room. Sleep still lingered, but her mind was busy thinking about yesterday. She felt her pulse quicken remembering the attic, the letters, and those spirits in love.

"Find the truth inside the witch's legacy," she whispered. What was the meaning? Her mind filled with memories of the light and whispers, each one sharp and clear. Then she thought of Marty, his laugh, and how strange things felt between them. She pushed her face into her pillow, trying to only think about his warm smile.

AT SCHOOL, the morning routine unfolded around her as it always did: lockers creaked open, shoes squeaked across the tiled floor, and the smell of freshly mopped halls lingered in the air. But Carson could hardly focus. The chatter around her faded, replaced by her own racing heart and swirling thoughts.

Just then, she spotted Marty leaning against a locker, casually tossing his backpack from one hand to the other. He caught her gaze, his warm brown eyes twinkling with mischief.

"Hey, Carson! Did you sleep in the attic last night?" he teased, his playful grin infectious. It was hard to resist, and her stomach fluttered with a mix of nerves and excitement.

"Very funny," she shot back, pretending to roll her eyes, yet feeling her cheeks warm.

"I wasn't scared at all, you know. If those ghosts come back, I'll protect you," he said, his tone light but somehow earnest, which sent a thrill through her.

"Right," she replied, trying to sound unimpressed. "You're so brave." Each word dripped with sarcasm, but the laughter that followed wasn't entirely fake.

Marty leaned closer, lowering his voice. "I'd take on any ghost for you, Carson." The sincerity in his eyes made her heart race. Just for that moment, she allowed herself to believe that yes, he really would protect her—against ghosts or any high school drama.

As the bell rang, signaling the start of class, Carson found it impossible to concentrate. The teacher's voice faded into a dull hum, replaced by the echo of Marty's words ringing in her ears. "I'll protect you."

She doodled absentmindedly in her notebook, spirals and shapes blending together, interspersed with sketches of Marty. One moment, she drew him smiling, tousled hair catching the light, and in the next, strings of letters floated above him, a ghostly love letter spilling out on the page.

Her mind raced back and forth between her feelings for Marty and the ghostly tale flourishing in the attic, her two worlds colliding in strange, tangled paths. It frustrated her and thrilled her at the same time.

At recess, she signaled to Milly, getting her to sidle over to a less crowded spot away from the bustling throng of students.

"Hey, did you think more about that curse?" Milly asked, her eyes lighting up with curiosity, blending perfectly with the excitement of discovery.

"I just can't shake it. I mean, Isolde's story—it was tragic," Carson replied, shifting her weight, uncertainty lingering. "What if we researched the history of witches? Maybe it'll lead us to clues about how to break it."

Milly nodded, her enthusiasm palpable. "That sounds like a solid plan! Let's dig into it online when we get home."

"Marty might want to join us too," Carson said cautiously. The thought of him being part of their research sent mixed signals through her.

Just then, Marty strolled up, catching the tail end of their conversation. "Did I hear something about witches? I'm in! I'd love to help you dig through all the juicy details."

Carson turned her head to hide her smile. "Right, because you're so interested in witch curses," she joked, but in truth, she appreciated his willingness to join.

"Hey, I'm just looking out for my favorite ghost hunter," he winked, and Carson could feel her stomach flutter again.

AFTER SCHOOL, the three of them made their way to the town library, the quiet ambiance enveloping them as they entered. Old books lined the wooden shelves, the scent of aged paper and ink filling the air, creating an almost magical atmosphere.

As they settled at an oak table, Carson's heart raced. The weight of what they were searching for pressed down on her like a thick blanket. Yet, seated next to Marty, that feeling of foreboding intertwined with excitement. Just as she opened a dusty volume on local folklore, she felt the familiar spark just from being near him—his presence wrapped her in warmth despite the chilling air of the library.

They all delved into their research, flipping through old newspapers and scanning handwritten notes, the silence broken only by the turning of pages. Carson felt more entwined in the ghosts' narrative with each passing minute, and her thoughts often wandered to the stories of love and heartache she was uncovering.

"Check this out," she suddenly called, running her fingers over an article that detailed ... Isolde's engagement to Sebastian Crowley. A sense of revelation washed over her. "This is why Isolde was upset. She was supposed to *marry* him, but then he fell for another woman!"

"Bastard," Milly whispered under her breath. "That's like, bad back then, right?"

Carson nodded her head, yes.

Marty leaned forward, intrigued. "What's the story here?"

Carson pointed to the words, her voice filled with tension. "This says that Isolde felt betrayed when she found out about Sebastian's affection for someone else. It makes everything more complicated. I thought he was innocent in all of this."

Milly frowned thoughtfully, catching Carson's eye. "So Isolde wasn't just some crazy jilted lover? She was hurt."

"Exactly," Carson murmured. The realization settled heavily in her chest, twisting like a knife.

Marty, sensing the shift in mood, broke the somber moment with a sly grin. "You know what they say about libraries, don't you? They're just full of people pretending to read while they really want to know about the latest gossip." That drew a reluctant smile from Carson, lightening the air a touch.

"Do they even have a library stereotype? Like, what is it—glasses, shushing people, and sipping tea?" Milly quipped, giggling.

As their laughter bubbled, Carson felt a spark of connection with Marty. But soon, the laughter faded, and her thoughts turned heavy again. "What would it feel like to be rejected by the man I loved?" she wondered, her mind racing with the implications. That dreadful thought sent chills down her spine. Would she be driven to such lengths as putting a curse on someone out of heartbreak?

Inspired by the discoveries and their shared laughter, Carson sat up straighter. "We need to perform a small ritual to honor Isolde and Sebastian, to help them find closure. Maybe it could give us the answers we need."

Milly's eyes lit up, and she nodded eagerly. "Whatever—I just want those noises—gone!"

Marty hesitated, furrowing his brow. "Is that really a good idea, Carson? What if something goes wrong?"

She met his gaze, determination rising within her. "I think we have to try. We owe it to them—to help them."

Their eyes lock and hold.

"Okay, fine. But I'm gonna be overprotective during this ritual, you know that right?" he replied half-joking, half-serious, his protective nature shining through.

Milly rolled her eyes. "Dude, that was lame."

Marty chuckled and extended his arms dramatically, "What?"

Milly sighed and gave him another eye roll. "You know exactly what."

8
nighttime

The Delgado Victorian home stood regally against the backdrop of twilight, its tall windows glowing softly like old lanterns welcoming the night. Shadows from the creaking branches of trees danced across the porch, lending an air of mystery to the historic façade. Inside, the atmosphere pulsed with anticipation.

Carson stayed back, sensing the energy that tingled beneath her skin, a mix of excitement and fear about what awaited her in the attic—a room filled with the unfulfilled love of two ghostly lovers and the lingering whispers of unresolved feelings.

She climbed the narrow, winding staircase, each step echoing in the quiet as if the house itself were holding its breath. Once inside the attic, Carson inhaled deeply, allowing the musty scent of aged wood and dust to fill her lungs. The dim light, flickering fitfully from the single bare bulb overhead, created a cozy yet eerie ambiance. It was here she would bridge the gap between the living and the dead, bridging two worlds with her intentions.

Carson carefully laid out her materials on the floor. The candles, their colors vibrant against the weathered wood, formed a small circle in the center of a delicate arrangement of flowers—wildflowers, gathered from outside, some vivid blues and soft yellows, embodying both love and remembrance. Pieces of paper lay nearby, ready for messages of closure. With trembling fingers, she took a moment, centering herself as her heart raced in sync with the anticipation building in her chest.

Carson looked up to see Milly hovering in the attic doorway, her face pale and her eyes wide with trepidation. The air seemed to thicken with tension as Milly's gaze swept over the candles, flowers, and Carson's makeshift altar.

"Whoa, this is...intense," Milly murmured, her voice wavering slightly.

Carson could sense the fear radiating from her best friend. Milly had always been the more adventurous one, but Carson understood the weight of the situation they found themselves in—reaching out to the spirit world was no trivial matter.

Marty appeared behind his sister, trying to mask his own apprehension with a casual shrug. "Come on, Milly, it's not that bad," he said, though his eyes betrayed a flicker of uncertainty. "Carson knows what she's doing."

Milly bit her lip, taking a tentative step into the room. "I know, but...it just feels so heavy in here." She swallowed hard, her gaze drawn to the flickering candles. "Like something's watching us."

Carson felt a pang of sympathy for her friend. She knew Milly was trying her best to be supportive, but the ghostly presence in the attic was palpable, even to those without Carson's heightened senses.

"Hey," Carson said softly, beckoning Milly closer. "It's okay to be scared. This is...intense, like you said. But I promise, I won't let anything happen to you."

Milly's shoulders relaxed slightly at Carson's words, and she managed a faint smile. "You always know how to make me feel better."

Marty stepped up beside his sister, wrapping a protective arm around her shoulders. "And you've got me here too," he added, his tone equal parts reassurance and bravado. "We're in this together, right?"

Carson nodded, grateful for Marty's steadying presence. She knew he was trying to be strong for Milly, but there was something in his eyes that betrayed his own curiosity—a desire to understand the supernatural forces at play.

"Right," Carson affirmed, her voice steadier than she felt. "We're a team. And if anyone can handle a couple of ghostly lovers, it's us."

Milly chuckled softly, some of the tension easing from her features. "Okay, you've got a point there." She took a deep breath, squaring her shoulders. "Let's do this, then."

Carson smiled, her heart swelling with affection for her two closest friends. They might not fully understand the depths of what she was about to attempt, but their unwavering support meant everything.

As Milly and Marty settled on the dusty floor beside her, Carson felt a renewed sense of determination. She had promised Sebastian and Celina that she would help them find closure, and with her friends by her side, she was ready to face whatever the night had in store.

Feeling a ripple of unease creep in, Carson whispered to herself, "I can do this." She lit the candles, watching the flames dance with an ethereal glow as if the spirits themselves rejoiced at the flickering light. Holding her breath, she focused inward, trying to connect with the energies surrounding her.

As she closed her eyes, the chill air thickened around her, wrapping around her like a shroud. The faint murmurs from the past echoed within her mind, emotions both sweet and bitter intertwining in a chaotic web. Carson felt a pulse of energy entering the space, her medium spirit tingling with recognition. For a moment, she felt their heartache, their restless love echoing through time.

"Sebastian, Celina," she called softly, her voice carrying sincerity and urgency. As she probed deeper, images flashed against the walls of her mind—moments of laughter, secret glances in shadowed corners, and whispered vows in hushed tones under the pale moonlight. She became their voice, channeling the aching love they had shared, the betrayal of time and fate. Each secret whisper poured from her lips in a symphony of longing.

Her emotions swelled with each word and flicker of the candles. The lovers seemed to control her, making her face their history and urge her forward. Their pain and strength turned into a nervous energy running through her body. She felt torn between lingering in this delicate instant and taking charge.

Yet just as she embraced their story—a crescendo of longing and sorrow—the atmosphere shifted abruptly. The door banged wide open, the sound jarring against the enchanted rhythm she'd established. Carson's eyes snapped open, and her heart plummeted at the sight of Sebastian standing there, pale and incandescent, his deep-set grey eyes brimming with surprise.

"Sebastian?" she exclaimed, shock slicing through her connection to the spirits.

His ethereal form flickered, casting wavering shadows against the attic walls. "Help us, Carson. Help us." His tone held urgency, but Carson felt only betrayal.

"You lied!" she spat, her voice louder than she intended, echoing in the stillness of the attic. "You led me to believe you were innocent in all this, that your love was nothing but pure." Anger coursed through her, fueled by the heartache she'd experienced while absorbing the couple's tragic tale.

Sebastian flinched, his eyes widening in surprise at her outburst. "Carson, wait! I—"

"No! Don't you dare pull me back into your web of deceit. You've hurt Isolde, and now you're trying to manipulate me as well?" Her breath came strangely fast, as the weight of their shared energy began to dissolve, threatening to send her back into isolation without resolution.

Sebastian shook his head, trying to find his words amidst the tempest of her emotions. "You don't understand. My love for Celina was real, but the circumstances—they were beyond my control. Isolde..." He hesitated, anguish tainting his voice. "She was lost in her obsession. She couldn't stand the thought of losing me. I didn't want to hurt her, but..."

"But you did! You chose Celina over Isolde, and now you're doomed to linger in this attic forever," Carson shot back, tears of frustration brimming in her eyes. She felt a deep connection to Isolde's pain, her heartache igniting a flicker of sorrow for the spirit she had yet to meet.

"Isolde? She can't be forgotten, Carson," Sebastian urged,

stepping closer. "If you complete this ritual, you'll not only free Celina and me but also help *her* find peace."

The air crackled around them, charged with tension as the other spirits faded. Carson's heart twisted at the thought of fracturing that delicate bond she felt with Sebastian and Celina. "You're already messing it up! Can't you see that?"

Sebastian's features softened, his voice flooding with sincerity. "I never meant for any of this to spiral out of control. I thought it was too late for Isolde; I didn't—"

Carson cut him off, the vision fading and turning to a distant haze. "Can you just feel the energy leaving?" she murmured, the reality hitting her like a tidal wave.

Suddenly, the candles flickered violently, throwing shadows that twisted grotesquely in the dim light. Tension hung thick in the air, a heaviness that pressed down on her chest. "Sebastian, you're breaking the connection!" Desperation clawed at her.

In that heavy moment, everything came together. Carson inhaled sharply, a final surge of determination compelling her forward. "For you to find closure, you need to apologize to Isolde," she declared, her voice steady but filled with emotion. "Your betrayal *hurt* her, and you can't find peace until you acknowledge that."

Sebastian's expression shifted, revealing regret masking vulnerability. Just as he opened his mouth to reply, the flames flickered and dimmed, shadows elongating ominously as fear gripped Carson.

Before she could draw another breath, a gust of wind slammed the attic door shut with a resounding thud. The candles sputtered and faltered, and a chilling whisper filled the air, echoing around them, entwining with the remnants of the spirit world.

"Milly!" The sound of her friend's voice faded as the atmosphere thickened.

"Carson! I don't like this!" Milly's voice echoed, distant and panicked, sending shivers down Carson's spine.

"Marty?" she called out, half in concern for her friend, half in desperation to hold on to someone who could save her from the maelstrom of spirit energy.

In the next breath, as if summoned from the shadows, Isolde appeared in a swirl of darkness and light, her long dark hair cascading like liquid silk, an unsettling beauty frozen in grief and rage.

Carson's heart raced as the reality of what stood before her twisted her stomach—a foreign spirit, poised to confront them.

9
who are you?

The attic hummed with a charged, electric tension as the last whisper faded into silence. Carson stood frozen, the lingering energy of the ritual knotting in her chest. She felt exhilaration coursing through her veins, but a gnawing anxiety lay just beneath the surface, threatening to bubble over. The presence of the spirits felt closer now, as if they were circling around her, beckoning her to engage with them more directly.

Carson's breath hitched. There stood Isolde Darkmoor, her dark hair cascading in waves down her back, wildflowers, now wilted and lifeless, entwined within the strands. She wore a flowing gown, tattered and suggestive of a bygone era. Isolde's green eyes glimmered with an intensity that sent prickles of fear racing down Carson's spine. The anger simmering beneath the surface was palpable, sparking curiosity mixed with dread.

In the stunned silence, the group felt the charged atmosphere closing in around them. Carson instinctively reached for Milly's hand, but before she could find comfort, Isolde's bitter voice sliced through the tension.

"You think it's so simple? You think you can just play with forces you don't understand?" The words dripped with venom, and the air shifted, drawing everyone's attention unapologetically to Isolde's piercing gaze.

Marty stepped closer to Carson, instinctively shielding her from the spirit's fury. His fingers brushed against hers, igniting a warmth that contrasted sharply with the chilly energy of Isolde. Carson's heart fluttered, caught between the flames of longing and fear.

"I'm okay," she managed to say, but the tremor in her voice betrayed her. The intimate touch lingered, if only for a moment, stirring something deeper within her.

Carson's heart raced as Isolde's gaze shifted to Milly, her expression shifting from rage to confusion. The atmosphere thickened, the weight of centuries of sorrow clinging like mist in the corners of the attic. Isolde's brows furrowed, mirroring the way their shared features danced in the dim light.

"And you?" Isolde's voice gained a cutting clarity. "Who are you? You bear my face... my eyes."

Milly stiffened beside Carson, her confidence faltering under the specter's scrutiny. "I—I'm Milly. Milly Delgado."

Delgado.

The name lingered in the air, rich with echoes of history, but it was the resemblance that sliced through Carson like a knife. Isolde's emerald gaze widened, searching Milly as if trying to dredge up memories buried deep.

"Delgado..." Isolde repeated, almost as if tasting the name. "I do not know the name. What manner of trickery is this? The same hair, the same eyes..." She took a step closer, a glimmer of desperation flitting across her face.

Carson felt the tension spiral. The question that clawed at her was almost unbearable. She stepped forward, wanting to bridge the chasm between the past and the present, her heart pounding with an ache to find clarity.

"She's related to you," Carson stated, her voice steady despite the uncertainty flooding her mind. "Somehow."

Milly glanced at Carson, her expression a mix of curiosity and apprehension. "What do you mean, somehow?"

Isolde remained focused on Milly, her frown deepening. "Related? By what bloodline?"

The question hung in the air, electrifying, as the implications twisted Carson's thoughts. She hesitated, searching for answers. *If Isolde never married Sebastian, then whom had she wed?* The realization danced just outside her comprehension, yet she kept it locked away, hidden alongside her own swirling uncertainties.

"A cousin, maybe?" Carson ventured, hating that an abyss of mystery surrounded her. She had hoped to discover the connectedness that danced along the tender edges of the human heart, yet she felt the brunt of an emotional weight building between them.

Carson threw a glance at Milly, who was visibly struggling to comprehend the full complexity of the moment. "What was your family's last name before marrying?" Isolde pressed, her voice dangerously low yet filled with an elegance that hinted at a tragic grace.

"We've always been Delgado," Milly replied, challenging Isolde's fierce gaze.

"But that's your father's last name," Carson said, turning towards Milly. "What's your mother's maiden name?"

Milly's face went white with shock when she realized the connection. "...I think her last name was Darkmoor."

Isolde's face contorted as if grappling with the implications of that statement. The weight of history bore down upon them, a tapestry woven of suffering and loss, love and regret. Carson felt the invisible seams fraying as she sought clarity through the fog of generations past.

"Then you bound yourself to the name of my fallacy. I left behind a legacy of pain, and far too many women followed my path in pursuit of love." Isolde's voice trembled with grief, her anguish pulling at the threads of Carson's heart. The memory of the love letters felt like an anchor anchoring her to the ethereal tale of ghostly lovers, as she watched Isolde's fierce spirit clash against that deep sadness.

Yet, swirling within Carson's thoughts was the other truth hovering in the shadows—if Isolde had not married Sebastian, then who had she wed? The question twirled illogically, unable to settle like a restless spirit. Part of her felt guilty for not voicing this revelation to Milly, but another part was terrified that voicing it would shatter the fragile connection they'd only just begun to forge.

"Don't you see how intricately connected we all are?" Isolde continued, her voice half pleading, half fierce. "The pain across our histories is the same—obsession, longing, separation. You have a choice before you, Milly. Will you continue the cycle, or will you break it?"

Milly flinched, and Carson tightened her grip on her friend's hand. "That's not fair—how can you expect her to choose a path she doesn't even understand yet?" Carson interjected, her voice laced with protective ferocity.

"Fair?" Isolde's lips curled into an unexpected smile that held both bitterness and sadness. "Love is not fair, young one. Love desires not fairness, nor clarity. It seeks only to bind and consume."

Carson stared into Isolde's haunting beauty, feeling the complexities of emotions stirring within her. The ache of longing, of understanding the past and the present, swirled together, forcing Carson to confront her own delicate feelings about Marty, about how deeply she desired to navigate the waters of love despite their turbulent nature.

"Look," Milly finally interjected, her voice shaking but steadying, catching both spirits off guard. "I want to help you—help you heal from whatever binds you here. But I'm not going to be trapped in someone else's story. I want my own life."

Carson's heart swelled at Milly's defiance, at her fierce determination to break free. Was this the thread she needed to untangle the chaos surrounding their shared lineage and Isolde's shadowed tale?

"What if I could help you break free?" Carson couldn't suppress her boldness any longer, feeling urgency seep into her bones. "You can tell us what we need to know."

Isolde paused, her gaze shifting to Carson with a glimmer of hope that faded into uncertainty. "You think you can comprehend the extent of what has been lost? Do you know how deeply love can wound?"

Carson swallowed hard, a knot of understanding forming in her throat. "I may not know what it's like to be bound by love as you were, but I can sense the sorrow surrounding it. I feel the weight of it all."

With that honesty, the atmosphere in the attic shifted again—an understanding blossomed amid the fear and confusion. It surged through the space like a wild wind, inviting possibilities she had previously kept at bay.

But what more would Isolde reveal about her past? Carson felt the compelling need to grasp every crumb of the story, each fragmented truth that could offer solace to Isolde and, perhaps, insights to guide Milly along her own journey.

The whispers of the attic swirled softly, resonating in their heavy silence, urging them toward greater revelations hiding in the shadows. Would they dare dive deeper into the echoes of love—the haunting legacy yet to be told?

"Do you wish to be buried alongside that legacy you can't escape?" Isolde's question pierced Carson's heart, an arrow aimed true amidst the confusion and intrigue.

10
listen to me

The attic glowed with flickering candlelight, casting dancing shadows across the walls. Each soft flicker created an intimate atmosphere, warmth mingling with the ghostly chill of the space, wrapping around the group like a comforting embrace. Whispers floated in the air, ethereal and elusive, swirling around Carson, Milly, and Marty like the remnants of forgotten dreams. It felt as if the very essence of the lovers' story coiled around them, binding them to this moment, this purpose.

As the delightful warmth enveloped them, Isolde's irate energy shattered the harmony. In an instant, she dissolved into a mist, leaving only a faint echo of her anger behind. The atmosphere shifted dramatically; just then, the ethereal forms of Sebastian and Celina re-materialized, their appearances a glittering counter to Isolde's stormy presence. Celina's shimmering white dress glowed softly, while Sebastian's melancholy figure held the weight of centuries of sorrow.

Carson inhaled sharply, her heart racing as a wave of emotions cascaded over her. She felt their stories flooding her mind—deep infatuations intertwined with despair. Love and heartbreak unspooled like ribbons of a forgotten tapestry. Images of a stolen kiss under a twilight sky accompanied the aching sound of a solemn lullaby that only she could hear. That heartbeat echoed her own, slipping into the background rhythms of her burgeoning feelings for Marty.

The feeling was intense but thrilling. She clutched the edge of the worn trunk beside her, bracing herself against the storm of emotions that threatened to overwhelm her. Each heartbeat heightened the connection she felt with the ghostly lovers, merging their pain with her own growing, unspoken feelings for Marty.

Sebastian stepped forward, his gray eyes shining with desperation. "Please," his voice trembled, "we need your forgiveness. I have done wrong to let our love be caught in this eternal web."

Celina's gentle presence lingered by his side as if reminding him of their shared burden. "We are trapped, bound by a curse that has lingered too long. We yearn to be free, not just for ourselves but for our future, your future."

Carson found herself lost in the depths of their eyes, her heart aching for their plight. "How can we help you?" she whispered, the intensity of their longing radiating towards her. The air thickened with emotion, reminding her of her own struggles for connection among the living.

Milly, ever the quick thinker, blinked as a thought struck her. "Wait!" She glanced back toward the books they had sifted through earlier. "I memorized something." Her gaze flickered between Carson and Marty, excitement bubbling within her. "In the library, I read a witch's spell. It might still work!"

"Are you sure?" Carson asked, a mix of anxiety and hope flaring within her. "Will it be enough?"

Milly nodded fervently, determination etched across her face, her brow furrowing in concentration.

"Okay, let's light a final candle to symbolize our intention," came Marty's voice, steady and calm, even amongst the swirling emotions.

They gathered around, arranging the candles and flowers Carson had previously prepared, creating a small altar of remembrance and hope that shimmered softly in the shadows.

Carson felt a renewed energy as she turned toward the spirits. "You're not alone," she said, her voice soothing and assured, echoing with strength as she spoke to the lovers. "Your love is recognized. It's honored here among the living."

With the trio gathered, Milly took a deep breath, feeling the weight of the moment. As she began to recite the spell from memory, the atmosphere shimmered with potential, the prospects of release dancing in the air.

However, before they could complete their ritual, a sudden wind swept through the attic, fierce and unforgiving. The candles flared wildly, spiraling flames shrinking until one by one, they extinguished, casting the room into profound darkness.

Fear gripped Carson's heart in that instant, a stark contrast to the exhilaration that had pulsed within her just moments before. The shadows thickened around them, creeping like fog, swirling around them in a possessive grasp.

"Damn it!" Marty muttered, his voice a mixture of surprise and uncertainty. The darkness felt heavy, filling the space where the spirit voices had once been. Carson gulped, trying to steady her racing heart.

Suddenly, Isolde erupted back into existence, her figure carved from the very shadows that cloaked the room. Her long, dark hair flowed wild, eyes blazing with fury as she took a step toward Sebastian. "You will listen to me now!" she demanded, her voice sharp and filled with intensity as it echoed through the emptiness.

A thrill of dread raced down Carson's spine. She sensed the urgency of their plight but knew that Isolde's arrival could throw them off-course. "Isolde, you're not helping!" she said quickly, trying to contain the escalating chaos that threatened to undo their efforts.

But Isolde paid no heed to her protest, her focus solely on Sebastian, who stood rigid, caught between the wrath directed at him and the love that tied them.

"I deserve to speak to you alone," she insisted, a fierceness akin to a tempest in her words.

As the winds howled around them, swirling remnants of past torments, Carson's breath quickened. They were standing on the precipice of something monumental, but would Isolde's anger unravel everything they'd worked toward? Would they be able to help Sebastian and Celina break free from the indescribable torment holding them captive?

Every heartbeat pulsed with uncertainty as they braced for the storm of emotions that would inevitably follow Isolde's demand.

Isolde stepped towards Sebastian, the weight of centuries of longing and bitterness swirling around her like a tempest. Her once-vibrant countenance had darkened, an intensity sparking in her green eyes as she confronted him. Silence stretched between them, heavy with unspoken grievances, the air practically crackled with anticipation.

"Why did you break our engagement?" Isolde's voice cut through the quiet, softer now yet brimming with wounded undertones. The transformation in her tone puzzled Carson, who stood frozen, sensing the pulse of unresolved emotions resonating in the room. A flicker of longing, desperation mingled with resentment danced across Isolde's features, illuminating the depths of her heartache.

Sebastian's shoulders tensed, his gaze drifting to the floor as if looking for a way out of the torment surrounding them. He seemed to weigh his words carefully, drawing an agonizing breath to quell the storm inside before answering. "Isolde," his voice trembled, ripe with regret, "it's not your fault. You did nothing wrong."

The sincerity in his tone was palpable. Isolde's expression flickered, the slightest crack appearing in her icy façade, just enough to glimpse the vulnerability beneath. Carson felt the energy shift again, the tension momentarily softening as they stared at one another, trapped in a dance of hurt and desperation.

"I was going to marry you," Sebastian continued, faltering as he met her gaze. "But then I met Celina… the night before."

The revelation hung heavy in the air. Carson's heart raced, and she exchanged a glance with Milly, the two sharing a silent understanding of the gravity of Sebastian's confession. Both were caught between their own emotional turmoil and the intimacy of the lovers' struggle.

"Celina?" Isolde echoed, her voice barely above a whisper, filled with a broken sweetness. Anger, hurt, and disbelief wove through her words as she reached for Sebastian, fingertips brushing against his chest, desperate to connect. "You met her before—after I offered you my heart?"

"Yes," Sebastian said, suppressing the guilt that swelled within him. "On that night, I had feelings I've never felt before. They—They scared me."

A tremor ran through the room, igniting a fresh wave of energy that sparkled in the air around them. Carson could feel the force growing; different than the earlier chaos, this burst softened hard hearts, making way for raw connection.

"Feelings?" Isolde's voice cracked slightly, her expression softening to something more vulnerable. "What kind of feelings?"

Sebastian's deep-set gray eyes shone with a mix of love and sorrow as he continued, undeterred. "With you, Isolde, it always felt… arranged—like it was about duty, something expected of me. Our love felt forced and loveless at times." Each word sank into the air, encased in the warmth of honesty that permeated the attic. "But with Celina… it was a connection I could no longer turn away from."

The truth hung tangible among them, palpable like the air thick with emotion. Isolde's breath hitched, sadness pooling in her eyes, and for a brief moment, the pain that clouded her was eclipsed by understanding. The fierce jealousy she masked had never extinguished; it now shimmered as an echo of longing, flickering against the backdrop of timeless despair.

"I'm sorry, Isolde," Sebastian's voice broke slightly as he took a tentative step closer, embodying the essence of humility and remorse. "I never meant to hurt you. I wish I could change what happened."

Isolde's eyes widened, shimmered like fading embers, reflecting both anger and sadness. "And yet, here we are," she said, her voice booming with both authority and fragility. "You turned away from me." The weight of heartbreak twisted in the air like a noose tightening around her spirit. "I can't merely forget."

Carson absorbed the raw emotions; she felt the heaviness of Isolde's pain coiling around her heart, tightening alongside the flutter in her chest that grew whenever she caught glimpses of Marty. She could sense the delicate balance of yearning and hurt, isolated but so achingly close.

Sebastian reached out, almost instinctively, letting his hand hover by Isolde's cheek, his spirit flickering pathetically. "I never wanted that. Forgiveness is all I seek now."

As he said these heartfelt words, Isolde's expression softened, confliction dancing in her features. Their shared history lingered between them, mingling with unfulfilled love, jealousy, and shattered promises. Carson held her breath, the delicate air thick; she wanted to will them together, to coax the darkness from their hearts.

Drawing a deep breath, Isolde suddenly recoiled, shaking her head as tears glistened in her eyes, shimmering like the ethereal forms they possessed. "My heart aches too much. I loved you, and I feel betrayed even now," she whispered, voice shaking. The rawness of her confession resonated throughout the room, a bittersweet melody that hung thick in the air.

As Sebastian stood torn between his former love and newfound connection, the spirits' energies around them began to change, like the clouds shifting before a storm. Carson couldn't shake the feeling that they were on the brink of something monumental, a release that transcended both realms.

With a firm resolve, Sebastian folded his hands into one another, grounding himself as he spoke. "Isolde, this curse binds us. Our pain must be lifted, not just for us but for your heart to heal too. We've lingered here in agony for so long."

In a gesture that felt vast and cosmic, Sebastian took a step back, orienting himself towards Celina. Their energies intertwined, weaving a tapestry of fate that Carson could sense. "I cannot undo what's been done, but I can let go. We can finally move on."

Celina floated beside him, her presence a shimmering glow that radiated magic and warmth. She leaned into Sebastian, compassion pouring from her gaze. "It is time, Isolde. Forgiveness does not mean forgetting, but it allows us to breathe."

With every word, Sebastian and Celina's forms began to shimmer, brightly lighting the dusky attic space. They faced each other, gliding effortlessly just above the ground, the weight of their sorrow lifting as hope swirled around them.

A luminous aura enveloped them, illuminating the attic with a breathtaking radiance. "Together, we will break this curse," Sebastian concluded, heart full of both sorrow and resolution.

As if on cue, their spirits began to float higher, first a few inches off the dusty floor, then drifting ever so gently upwards, approaching the beams of the attic. Their forms melded seamlessly with the light surrounding them, the air tinged with both wonder and heartache.

Carson watched with bated breath, struck by the beauty unfolding before her. The shadows that had once claimed the room now yielded to pure light, and as Sebastian and Celina ascended into the sky like two stars being released into the night, they dissipated into fragments of the past, their lingering love echoing in the air.

"Forgive me—" Isolde whispered, her voice trembling as she finally metamorphosed from bitter anger into bittersweet acceptance.

The radiant forms of Sebastian and Celina soared higher and higher, disappearing from view, leaving behind a faint shimmer as though the miracle of their love ignited something divine.

Just like that, the spirits transcended the mortal realm, and with their departure, the sins and sorrows that bound them began to unravel, lighting the way for Isolde to come to terms with her heartache.

11
chaos

The attic plunged into darkness, enveloping Carson, Milly, and Marty in an unsettling silence. The soft flicker of candles disappeared as shadows swirled around them, amplifying the sensation that something powerful lay just beyond their senses. Heartbeats quickened, tension hanging thick in the air, mixing fear and urgency like the eerie whispers that danced through the night.

"What just happened?" Milly's voice echoed in the void, her breath quickening as she struggled to comprehend the sudden shift.

"Let me get my phone," Carson murmured, fumbling for her phone in her pocket. Her fingers trembled as she swiped the screen, beams of light illuminating their anxious faces. She directed the beam towards the walls, revealing dust motes floating aimlessly in the flickering light.

Marty moved closer, the warmth of his presence grounding her amidst the chaos. "We need to see what's going on," he urged, his voice steady despite the rush of adrenaline.

The gust of wind echoed again, weaving through the attic like a presence of its own, carrying with it whispers that prickled the base of Carson's spine. She squeezed her eyes shut, attempting to drown out the fear and listen to the messages from the spirits, her heart resonating with their desperate need for resolution.

"Marty, stay close," Carson whispered, her voice feeling fragile in the overwhelming darkness. The weight of uncertainty surged through her, mingling with visions of the ghostly couple and their tangled fate.

With his hand falling protectively on her shoulder, sparks of electricity flew between them, deepening their connection. She felt her pulse race with the mix of fear and warmth radiating from him, adding a layer of comfort amidst the storm.

Gathering herself, Carson steeled her resolve, "We need to focus on Isolde."

Milly nodded, her determined expression illuminated by the faint glow of Carson's flashlight. Together, their solidarity emboldened Carson as she spoke aloud, breaking through the darkness clinging to their hopes. "Isolde, if you're here, we want to help."

As if summoned by her words, the energy in the room shifted; the air thickened, filled with anticipation. "How can you help me?" Isolde's voice, now intermingled with eerie winds, echoed through the attic like the scorn of a tempestuous spirit.

Before Carson could respond, an unexpected crash echoed from the far corner of the room. They all jumped, instinctively moving closer together as a trunk creaked open, its hinges groaning in protest. Amidst the darkness, the trunk revealed a sprawl of letters and artifacts, hinting at layers of Sebastian and Celina's tragic love they had yet to uncover.

"I'll read them," Carson declared, moving toward the open trunk, her heart racing with both fear and excitement. She began to sift through the contents, pulling out weathered letters tied with fraying ribbons. As she read aloud, dark secrets poured forth, steeped in jealousy and betrayal, casting a new light on the lovers' story.

Tension curled around them as bursts of specter energy flickered in response. Each revelation dripped with the sorrow of unfulfilled dreams, displaying the raw power of love and loss.

Suddenly, Isolde's fierce presence surged like a summer storm, her anger palpable. "It was my jealousy that led to the curse!" she exclaimed, her desperate tone unwavering. "I wanted Sebastian for myself, and in my desire to protect my love from rejection, I doomed us all!"

Deep within Carson's heart, the understanding bloomed like a flower—Isolde was not merely the antagonist but a tragic figure shaped by her own mistakes. The brimming emotions of betrayal and longing wrapped around them, casting a shadow over their feelings about love.

"But, we're related!" Milly exclaimed, her eyes wide with discovery. "Don't give up!" She drew their attention to another letter, revealing a hidden incantation, one that resonated with potential. "Look," Milly explained, her voice trembling. "We need to find something dear to the one in love."

Carson swallowed hard; her mind raced as she contemplated the implications. "Like what? She's been dead for hundreds of years."

"Wait," Milly continued, fishing through her backpack. "I found something the other day," she produced a beautiful necklace, sparkling faintly even in the dark. "It belonged to my great-great-grandmother. I always thought it was just a family trinket. Maybe it can help balance the energies!"

Hope and trepidation flickered between them, igniting the possibility of the ritual taking form. With the necklace in hand, they shared a collective determination as they prepped for the incantation, gathering their energies to move forward.

"Isolde," Carson called, her voice steady. "If you want to be free, help us. We can do this together."

Energy pulsed in the attic, swirling around them. Flickering lights began to materialize, illuminating the specters hovering nearby. Each figure carried remnants of unresolved emotions, wading through memories that intertwined, revealing glimpses of the past.

Milly whispered, "We can break the curse."

But just as they began to chant, Isolde exploded into anger. "You think you can rewrite fate?"

The winds rose violently, creating a maelstrom of chaos. Objects began flying across the attic, crashing into walls and sending dust spiraling into the air.

With the swirling energies colliding around them, the very fabric of the atmosphere crackled with intensity. Carson squeezed the necklace in her hand, heart pounding as she stepped forward. This was not just an act for the spirits—it was an act of courage.

Marty watched her, uncertainty in his gaze. "Carson, are you—"

"Trust me," she whispered, drawing strength from him and Milly. They stood united, aware of the stakes at play.

With resolve etched on her face, Carson extended the necklace toward Isolde. "Take it. Use it to find your peace, to finally break free."

As she relinquished the necklace, it shimmered with a brilliant light—the culmination of love, loss, and sacrifice melding into a singular moment.

"Perhaps love is less of a curse than a lesson," she whispered—caught in a dazzling brilliance—her voice fading like mist as she dissolved into the ether.

Amidst the chaos, a calm swept through the attic, leaving only the soft glow of the spirits intertwined—a final testament to love's enduring power. Carson stood grounded, heart racing, acutely aware of the transcendent journey that lay ahead.

12
love entwined

The fading sun cast a golden glow over the park, suffusing the scene with warmth as Carson, Milly, and Marty settled onto their favorite bench beneath a sprawling oak. This was their sanctuary, a place where laughter and memories intertwined with the rustling leaves and the scent of freshly mowed grass. The trio shared a moment of quietness, allowing the last rays of light to wrap around them, reflecting on the recent turbulent events they'd navigated together.

Milly leaned back, inhaling the sweet scent of the blooming flowers nearby. "Can you believe how far we've come? From ghost adventures to...ta-da! Ice cream at sunset!" She waved a spoon in exaggerated excitement, a smile breaking across her face.

"Yeah, we survived curses, drama, and still managed to get ice cream," Carson chuckled, her heart lighter than it had been in weeks. The collective weight of their experiences had somehow strengthened their friendship, binding them together with resilient threads of support.

Marty dipped his cone into a pool of melted chocolate, smirking as he took a big bite. "I'd say battling vengeful spirits and learning about cursed lovers is quite the summer activity," he laughed. "I hope next time it's a little less... traumatic."

"Agreed," Carson said, her eyes sparkling with warmth. "But honestly? Those moments taught me so much about myself. I felt so lost with my medium abilities—like I was drifting always in the shadows. Now I feel more in tune with who I am." She let out a sigh, contemplating how much her journey had impacted them all.

"It's like we're ghost hunters and life guides at the same time. Who knew this was a dual career?" Milly interjected, indulging in her ice cream. The light-hearted banter resonated, bringing Carson back to the joy of their camaraderie.

They shared stories about the ghostly lovers, reminiscing about the nights spent in the attic, attempting to find closure for Sebastian, Celina, and Isolde.

"I just hope Isolde found some peace. She was intense. She deserved closure, too," Marty stated, his voice shifting solemn.

"Right? And I wonder who she eventually married," Carson mused, her mind tracing back to the letters they found. "Did she ever really move on?"

"Let's be real for a second," Milly interrupted, her teasing tone returning, "The likelihood of a lady in her era getting a second chance at love seems pretty slim. That's like bad luck squared."

"I guess some love stories never end happily," Carson remarked, but a smile danced on her lips, spreading warmth from within.

"But that doesn't make sense," Milly interjected again. "If Isolde never married, then how are *we* related to her?"

Carson looked up from licking her ice cream. "She must have married, right?"

"She had to have," Marty concluded.

As the sun dipped further, casting the park in hues of violet and rose, Marty turned serious. He took Carson's hand, the warmth radiating from his touch sending a flutter through her chest.

"Carson," he began, his eyes meeting hers with an intensity that pushed the noise of the outside world away. "You mean so much to me. I want... no, I need to explore what this is between us—a relationship that isn't just friends anymore."

Carson's heart raced at the sincerity in his gaze. She felt the weight of her shared experiences with him—their laughter, their fears, the moments they'd bridged the gaps between them. It was thrilling, yet terrifying all at once.

Milly feigned a dramatic gasp, breaking the intensity. "Oh no! He's going to confess his undying love! What will we do?" she interjected, rolling her eyes but unable to keep the smile from her face.

"Come on, you know it's not like that." Marty laughed softly, but his eyes still lingered on Carson.

"Actually, I think it's exactly like that," Carson replied, her heart urging her to reciprocate. "I'd love to see where this goes, Marty. I—I feel like I'm finally ready." The words felt freeing, opening up a door to a future filled with possibility while shedding the weight of the ghosts they encountered.

As twilight descended, embracing them in its cozy ambiance, laughter erupted soon after, intertwined with newfound ease. The worries of the past felt distant, swallowed by the friendship and budding romance they were forging.

"Do you think we'll find more stories?" Milly asked, finishing her cone with a satisfied sigh.

"Definitely," Carson replied, "There are always more tales of love and loss waiting to be discovered. We'll create our bucket list for ghost-hunting!"

Marty looked beyond them, as if contemplating future adventures. "Let's make it a tradition," he suggested enthusiastically.

Just as they stood to leave, Carson's gaze fell to the ground where something glimmered in the dim light. She knelt down, revealing a small charm—a delicate stone etched with swirling patterns, exuding a faint energy. "Hey, look at this!"

"Just a little keepsake to remind us of our ghostly friends?" Milly teased, but there was a sincerity in her voice as she picked up the charm. "Circle of life, yeah?"

"Exactly," Carson affirmed, feeling a surge of closure wash over her. It felt like a punctuation mark on their intertwined journeys, seeping slowly into something deeper—something that would forever connect them to Sebastian, Celina, and Isolde.

Carson pocketed the charm, her heart swelling with the promise of new adventures, friendships, and a flicker of hope for love. The evening air filled with laughter as they took the long way home, wrapped in the new warmth of connection.

AS CARSON SETTLED into her favorite nook on the floor of her bedroom later that night, she spread open her journal, positioned perfectly by the glow of her bedside lamp.

She fingered through her reflections, her heart resonating with everything she had experienced—the lessons learned, ghosts released, and newfound confidences blossoming. Surely all of this shaped her into someone stronger, someone who could help others navigate their own spectral burdens.

Carson placed the charm down next to her journal while her pen glided across the pages, tracing musings of the past—old love tales and her growing role as a medium, guiding lost souls toward closure, a responsibility she felt she could honor.

But just as she wrote the final words, a chill seeped into the room, lifting the hairs on her arms. The air thickened, palpable, filled with unyielding energy that tugged at her consciousness.

A figure emerged from the shadows, flickering and flickering into shape. Carson's breath caught in her throat, eyes widening. This new spirit held an unmistakable urgency—a man with striking features and an air of desperation.

"Isolde..." The name fell from his lips, permeating the air with sorrow, carrying the weight of history untold. His voice, thick with emotion, hung in the atmosphere like a heavy fog. "Help me find her..."

Isolde? Carson thought, her mind racing. *Does he know her?* "How do you know Isolde?"

The spirit held his hat in his hands, fingers trembling as he clutched it tightly, a gesture of both reverence and desperation. "She's my wife."

Carson's heart plummeted to the pit of her stomach, a jolt of shock coursing through her. *His wife?* The revelation sent a shiver down her spine. "And you are? What is your name?" She couldn't shake the feeling that the answer would unravel more than just this ghost's identity.

"McBride," he replied softly, his voice barely above a whisper. "Patrick McBride."

Patrick?! The name echoed in her thoughts, a whirlwind of confusion and recognition colliding within her. Carson's breath caught in her throat as she processed the revelation. *That's my grandpa's name!* The connection felt electric, bridging the gap between the past and her present.

Carson then grabbed her cell phone and immediately sent a text to her best friend.

> U R NOT gonna believe this!

THE END

journey to crystal lake - part one

escape the ordinary. find your spark.

Get swept away with Journey to Crystal Lake, a thrilling YA romance in two parts!

Maddie's annual camping trip takes a dramatic turn when a blizzard tears through the mountains, separating her from her family. Lost and alone, she finds herself in a deserted cabin... with Dex, the infuriatingly handsome boy from school who secretly holds her heart.

Will they find their way back together, or will the storm ignite a bitterness even fiercer than the blizzard?

Part One!
Young Adult Romance
by Lia Lucas
Ebook & Paperback

haunted hearts

a summer camp. a tragic past. a ghost with an unfulfilled longing.

Can you feel a chill?

Riley thought summer camp would be filled with friends, campfires, and maybe a little flirting. But when she arrives at the rumored haunted camp, she discovers a secret world beyond her wildest imagination. There, she encounters the ghost of a dashing young counselor, trapped between the living and the dead.

As their connection deepens, Riley must navigate the complexities of a forbidden love while unraveling the chilling mystery surrounding the ghost's tragic demise. Will their love story be a haunting memory or a chance for redemption?

Prepare to be captivated by a tale of love, loss, and the supernatural.

Young Adult Romance

Ebook & Paperback

about lia

Lia Lucas is an emerging author of Urban Fiction, Young Adult, and Contemporary Romance. She has a wide range of writing interests and is currently living an incognito digital lifestyle.

Ms. Lucas is part of the Ardent Artist Books family.

Lia has published several books.

youtube.com/theardentartist
amazon.com/stores/Ardent-Artist-Books/author/B08BX8F1DZ

also by lia

YOUNG ♦ ADULT

Journey To Crystal Lake - Part One

Snowbound with the Boy Next Door - Part Two

Star-Crossed Rivals

SERIES

The Haunted Hearts Series

Haunted Hearts - Book 1

Ink and Ashes - Book 2

Ghosts in the Attic - Book 3

18+ ♦ Adult

Curves

She Was Going Home

www.ingramcontent.com/pod-product-compliance
Lightning Source LLC
LaVergne TN
LVHW021225080526
838199LV00089B/5828